THIS
TIME
OF
YEAR

—DANIEL CASEY—

Cover design by Jill Giulietti
Book design by The Troy Book Makers
Printed in the United States of America
The Troy Book Makers • Troy, New York • thetroybookmakers.com

To order additional copies of this title,
contact your favorite local bookstore
or visit www.shoptbmbooks.com

ISBN: 978-1-61468-850-1

In memory of Helen M. Casey and Jean Bufe Purdy
Gone but not forgotten.

LATE NIGHT RADIO

Ken Heet often thought about the old days and with the state of affairs in the world, he was not alone. The wheels were coming off. Things were turning upside down here, there, and everywhere. A forward-looking person would try to diagnose the upheaval and suggest possible solutions. Ken preferred to look in the rearview mirror to a better time. Yes, the old days had been something for the "peaked in high school" type of guy. For him, the 1980s were the prime years. Bring on long hair, loud music, and underpowered Camaros with T-Top sunroofs. Man, those were the days. Back then, hi-tech was a CD player, but he had held onto his vinyl and cassette tape collection. He still had the collection in storage. It might have value down the road. Oh, to go back, if only for a short while.

Ken worked the overnight shift at a parcel sorting center. He was a tenured, full-time employee of Global Transport Company (GTC) and a proud Teamster. The bulk of his duty was to shuttle trailers around in preparation for the morning runs. A mundane job for sure. What really got his wheels turning was late-night talk radio. The shows eased the monotony with "scientific" discussions on UFOs, assorted conspiracies, ghost stories, and one of his favorite topics, time travel and the possibility of rolling back through the years.

Ken didn't fully grasp the theories discussed, and when some of the more sketchy callers phoned in, things could get chaotic. The far-out calls were a distraction from the flow of the discussions. When the shows got off track, Ken would get distracted with thoughts drifting back to a time when he took the field. "Bring on the Heet." He could still hear the cheers echoing through the crowd for the star running back. Those crowds were large, even when the weather turned cold.

Football was a popular sport at Colonial High. Ken was on the cusp of being good enough to play at the collegiate level. But things didn't work out, not an uncommon experience. There are hundreds of also-rans scattered across varsity squads at the end of every season. Now, many years later, here he sat waiting to hook up the next trailer to his rig and line it up for the day shift to move along. A robot, or some other AI system, could do this job and likely would someday. Ken Heet could be out of the game again, but this time without a paycheck. That pothole was down the road, and yet another reason to look back to the past. Who knew what workforce shake-up was coming?

Should his financial situation sour, he would have one less worry than some of his co-workers. He had remained single despite dating over the years and had no extra mouths to feed. With the way things were going for him and the world, he figured it was a good decision. He only had to fend for himself, spared the stress folks with families carried every day. Those memories of the good old days were more powerful with little else to think about.

Nightwork is not conducive to new romance. If one enters the midnight shift unattached, with no love life, the chance of finding a soul mate goes down. Ken stayed on the shift for a few reasons, one being extra pay. The union had negotiated a bump in pay for the night shift. Extra compensation was provided for the vampire-like existence. With that factored into his union wage, he made more than enough for a single man in modest housing. Additionally, the shift was generally quiet, run by a good supervisor, Bill Powers, a boss who looked out for his people. Being senior on the shift, Ken had his choice of vacation days. He would lose that seniority moving to days. The last reason he lingered on the overnight shift wasn't something he cared to admit. It was a not-so-subliminal justification. The work schedule allowed him to hide. He, and his family, had expected more. Most of his friends had worked their way into lives full of accomplishments at the family level and professionally. Not so much for Ken. The graveyard shift kept him out of sight. He hung low, hiding in the dark with talk radio keeping him company. The host and the guests didn't judge him. As Ken Heet wandered into his thirties, he wondered if this was how the next thirty years would go. A numbing thought for sure.

* * *

Across the Globe was the nationally syndicated radio program Ken enjoyed the most. It started at midnight and kept him company for the bulk of his shift. His companions consisted of many oddballs, some probably certifiable nuts. That was not the politically correct terminology of the day, but it had been the lingo when Ken came of age. "Nuts" was a common slang term, nothing personal, no offense meant. Mixed in among the nuts were some interesting guests and a likable host. David Sphere was the ringmaster on the air. Ken doubted that was the host's real name, but it fit the show. The host handled the wacky call-in characters politely and came across as a sincere, friendly fellow. His voice was perfect for radio, clear and smooth-toned. He wasn't offensive as shock jocks tended to be, filled with bravado and hubris but few accomplishments to back up their bluster. David Sphere was quite the opposite, and Ken came to view him as a good friend he never actually met.

Discussions often revolved around the paranormal with UFOs a frequent theme. Initially somewhat interesting, the extraterrestrial tales became repetitive, featuring many of the same incidents and same callers, rehashing pseudo-events. Was other life out there other than what stomps around Earth? Ken figured it was possible, if not probable. There is a huge universe mostly unexplored. What were the odds of this planet being the only inhabitable spot in such a huge area? If there was someone or something else out there, so be it. How the heck was it affecting him? Nobody descended from the stars to his lonely rig to abduct him. He figured if aliens did come down, they would turn around and beat feet; this place was a mess.

"White noise," or the ghost story, was another recurring genre. That also didn't do much for Ken. Creepy, with occasionally interesting tales, but again no personal effect. There weren't any listless departed souls bothering him. As the saying goes, "All politics is local." We care about what affects us. Of course, no late show is complete without conspiracy theories, and Ken had heard scores of those. Some fascinating, others mildly interesting, and some bizarre. Topics of those discussions varied from assassinations to the cause of wars and a legion of other worst-case scenarios.

Time travel was the subject that caught his attention but wasn't covered often, with only an occasional segment delving into the issue. Ken had never given it much, if any, consideration until listening to *Across the Globe*. It was confusing, but intriguing to a man like Ken Heet, who was beginning to believe his best days were behind him.

There are various reasons why a person may long to go back in time. Perhaps to take something back, some ill-advised words that had caused irreparable harm. Or a parent who longed to return if only for a minute, to pick up and hug their children who had grown up and were out in the world. If they had known how fast it went by, they would have taken more time to do it when the kids were young. Ken, with no children, did not have those thoughts. For him, the trip back would be purely based on nostalgia, to a time when things were simple, more fun. As it was now, time was standing still for Ken Heet.

The world of late-night radio gave Ken something to ponder as he sat in the cab of an old rig, the diesel engine growling. He was growing older by the hour and day. Time was slipping by. Was it possible? Could one go back for a visit?

POSSIBLE IN THEORY

Until listening to David Sphere's program, Ken never believed the theory of time travel had any validity. He thought it was a joke. As a kid he had seen movies and TV shows that delved into the subject. There was H.G. Wells and his Time Machine, but Ken figured that was purely entertainment, along the lines of Star Trek. It wasn't until Sphere and his guests delved into the topic of "intense gravitational acceleration" and travel by speed of light that Ken learned there were scholarly adherents to the theory. According to Sphere's guests, many of whom held advanced degrees in astrophysics and the like, it was possible to travel through time, at least in theory. However, these experts said current technology would not get the job done. We can't move people or objects at the speed of light. There is no Millennium Falcon, from Star Wars fame, waiting to move us about at light speed.

According to the professors, it would be a one-way trip – forward but not back. Going ahead in time was of little interest to Ken. Why the heck would he want to go into the future in a world getting wackier every day? Besides, on his current track of life skipping forward twenty years, he would likely see himself as an old-timer driving a truck. At best he would be supervising others doing the same. Ken would be the replacement for his beloved boss Bill Powers, who would by then have walked off into retirement. It was the past, the good old days, that captured Ken's interest. Man, if only for a day or so.

There was one scholarly guest on Sphere's show who explained the Einstein-Rosen Bridge Theory. Albert Einstein said it was possible to build, or take, bridges to the past. This involved "wormholes." What exactly they were Ken could not quite grasp. However, he knew who Albert Einstein was, a heavy name in the world of science for sure. The details confused Ken who had skated out of high school science class, but if a genius said it was possible, there must be something to it. This theory was much harder to grasp than the speed-of-light scenario proposed for traveling forward in time. Ken Heet's attention span was not suited for theories involving wormholes or black holes. Listening to the theories discussed on the radio was akin to science class. His thoughts back in high school would have drifted to an upcoming game, or the party afterwards. His teachers took it easy on him. They knew he carried the football team. The faculty would have had to listen to the cries of the coaches, and possibly the athletic director, if one of their star athletes was determined to be academically disqualified for even one game, let alone an entire season. It helped that Ken was cordial, showed up on time for class, and would work with a tutor to get through the more challenging subjects. He did what was required to pass and remain eligible to play. His most challenging classroom endeavor to this point had been obtaining his Class A license, granting him commercial driver's status and a livelihood.

Ken wasn't about to delve into extra reading or research on the possibility of kicking around in time. He would listen to the experts on *Across the Globe* and take their word for it. Sphere would open the call-in lines and put a damper on things when they got too spaced out.

"Hello Jake from Albuquerque, you are on live. What is your question or comment?"

"Hi David, thanks for taking my call, longtime listener. I will tell you I have experiences with time travel. I made it back to the time of Napoleon. I got to see the man, and he wasn't such a bad guy, not as short as you think…"

Ken would then say to himself, "What the hell! Are these the type of people I am listening with? Am I nuts?" David Sphere would screen out the real wild ones, but some oddball always seemed to get through offering comic relief for the listeners. After all, it was 3 a.m. This was to be expected.

What really intrigued Ken was the "grandfather paradox" as described by a guest whose comments Ken found interesting. If you go back in time and cause the death, intentionally or not, of your grandfather before your father was born, how is it possible that you were alive to go back in time to begin with? That was a morbid scenario. Ken loved his grandfather and grandmother. The thought of causing death to either of them was the creepiest of scenarios. He often wondered how his own father turned out so dour, with such a jovial dad of his own. Grandpa Joe would be at the top of the list of people Ken would like to see again. He died shortly after Ken graduated from Colonial High.

Still, the theory was thought-provoking. You don't want to open Pandora's box and unleash a string of events with dire results. What if Ken traveled back and made small adjustments? Perhaps choosing a different course of study, spending less time playing sports, more time hitting the books. Maybe seeking out a different girlfriend, expanding the dating circle a bit. With no kids of his own, it wasn't as if he would be removing people from existence. Unless of course the new girl he hooked up with had kids now, in the present, and he stole her from her would-be husband. Did he really want to play around with events in the past? Ken was just turning the wheels of thought. If a person went back, it is likely not much would change. You are who you are and probably would relive the same experiences. From a personal standpoint, things weren't so bad for Ken. He was doing better than some of his old compatriots. Things could be much worse.

Ken would be the first to admit he wasn't a big thinker. Keeping it cut and dry worked fine for him. The real interest in time travel for him centered around it being fun. He would be hitting the replay button on hopping times. Maybe sneak in one more run down the field under the lights. Just a taste of the old life would be a hoot. No cell phones, no email, no internet at all. Back in those days people still talked face to face as a means of communication. No texting or on line chatting, you carried on conversations with people throughout the day. Everyone didn't have their mugs buried in a screen. If it was buried in anything, it was a book, written print. There were things called encyclopedias, which required a little diligence, sifting through the pages to find out what you want to know. It wasn't all great. They were near the end of the Cold War, so nuclear annihilation was still an existential threat, but after so many years that looming worst-case scenario was a fact of life.

Just to go back and romp around for a bit, see some old friends, a few who were gone, having died young. Perhaps meet some new ones, talk to people you never took the time to meet, get out of the clique you were in, expand your horizons. Even if time travel was unattainable, pure fiction, it doesn't hurt to dream. High hopes can help a person keep moving along as they trudge through life.

CHRISTMAS EVE OVERTIME

Ken was quick to come in early or stay late for overtime, with holidays being a favorite. This night's rate would be double time, holiday pay. He hated to pass it up. Far from greedy, he just didn't like the idea of turning money down, tax rate be damned. Sure, Uncle Sam took more than his fair share of the overtime pay, but it was still found money in Ken's eyes. With neither wife nor kids at home, holidays and school events weren't a priority. His schedule was wide open.

Bill Powers appreciated workers like Ken. They stepped up and took the hours others didn't want. Powers hated to make it mandatory for his people to work holiday shifts. Ken helped alleviate those situations by taking all the hours he could. On this Christmas Eve, Bill himself was working with his favorite go-to guy for holiday OT. Bill's kids were grown and out of the house, so he had no qualms about covering for the parents with young ones. They should be at home on Christmas Eve.

"Thanks again, Ken. I was close to mandating someone this year, but you, me, and a few others will make it work. A skeleton shift, but we will get it done. We should even be able to get out an hour or so early. The weather looks like it is winding down."

A wintery mix had coated the local roads and was slowing things down at the depot. Typical for the Northeast, ice had built up, then snow came to cover the ice. You had to be very careful when driving or walking on that treacherous surface.

"No problem, Bill. This storm isn't too bad. We will take our time, and all will be good."

They were discussing the game plan for the night in the break room with a handful of others. As expected, they were short on staff this shift. After assignments were given, all cleared out except for Ken and Bill, who liked to chat it up. Ken viewed Bill as a father figure, having liked him from the first day they met five years back. Bill Powers had a grandfatherly look with thick gray hair. He maintained a lean build from all the moving around at work. Ken hoped he would hold up as well. So far, he was doing so, not too far off from his playing weight. He worked out regularly maintaining an almost boyish appearance.

"So, Ken, what are you doing with all the money you are raking in with the overtime hours?"

"Stocking it away. It's my rainy-day fund. Truth

be told, I don't have much going on these days. I figure why turn down the money. I would be sitting home."

"Well, it is smart that I don't see you rolling in here with a hot ride like so many of the other guys. Those trucks come with big payments. Some of these dudes pay $600-$800 a month for the trucks and cars they tool around in. That's what my first mortgage payment was."

"They are pissing away money. I may get a house soon, but for now I have a great deal on my apartment. I don't lean on the landlord for repairs, so the rent stays the same. The place is quiet. Nobody bothers me."

"If you get a house, you gonna live there alone?" Bill said that coyly. He had been ribbing Ken about getting a steady girlfriend for a while.

"There isn't anybody else to move in except my dog."

"You don't get a bit lonely over there?" Bill flashed a small smile. Ken had seen the smirk before.

"I am doing all right, Bill. Nobody is chasing me for money and the cops aren't after me." This said with a wink.

"Ken, whenever I hear someone say, 'I don't know where I would be if I didn't meet my wife,' I think to myself, I know exactly where I would be or have been — belly up to a bar. If she hadn't come along, things would not have turned out well, that I can tell you. I was a lost boy."

"Yeah, well I'm not belly up to the bar, and I show up to cover overtime shifts for you."

They both laughed. It was a continuation of the not-so-subtle encouragement Bill pushed on Ken. The way he saw it, people like Ken should be the ones getting married and having children, the responsible folks of the world.

"I know I kid you, Ken, but I respect your hesitation. It is a huge decision. I have seen a lot of people rush into it, marriage and kids. Things can go off the rails quickly. It is a huge decision. When things turn bad and the kids get stuck in the middle, there are no winners. It is sad, tragic really. Your time will come, Ken, although if I had a daughter, I just might be pushing her your way."

"Only if she was cute!"

"Ha, it's in the eyes of the beholder my friend."

"Well, Bill, I do think we have some work to do."

"Ain't I the one who is supposed to be telling you that?"

* * *

Christmas time is always exceptionally busy in the parcel-delivery business. The system is overloaded. Ken Heet and his co-workers had been going full tilt for weeks. This night was no exception. These packages would be a little late; Santa missed the deadline. The storm made matters worse. The company plow had not cleared the pavement of snow. An underbelly of ice had built on the ground as well as the trailer tops.

"Bill, we are going to have a problem moving around out here. I am slipping badly, having a hard time hooking up the trailers." Ken was using the in-house portable radios to communicate with his supervisor.

"Received, Ken, I'll be out to give you a hand."

The mess on the trailers would have to be removed before they hit the road. That was the law. The lot had a snow rake for that. It was a large, elevated bar, but it was stationary. The trailers had to be hooked up first and moved to the rake station. Ken was not getting on the main roads tonight. He was staying in the lot, but the trucks had to be ready for the next scheduled working day. Hooking up the trailers would not be easy. Usually, the lot would be plowed sufficiently to move the trucks and trailers around. Tonight, with a limited crew on hand, that job was not done.

When Bill arrived, Ken was shoveling the snow and ice in the area where the tractor would back up and latch onto the trailer.

"Bill, I have cleared most of it out. If you can back it up, I'll deal with any more snow and get you in. I know you can still drive. You've been at it a lot longer."

Ken was not about to tell his supervisor to start shoveling. The heavy lifting should always go to the younger people on the crew, certainly not the supervisor.

"I think I can handle it, wise-ass, although I may have to go in a little fast to get through the snow."

The first try was a bust. Bill nearly got stuck.

"Ken, do you want me to call the plow truck over?"

"No, let him work the other side of the lot. You almost have it. I'll clear some more snow. If you give it a little more gas you should slide in and lock on. We may need the plow to get us out though. We will see."

The next attempt Bill did indeed give it more gas. He rammed through the snow and slammed into the trailer for a solid connection while Ken stood off to the side. Bill gave it a bit too much throttle. He locked in with so much force that ice flew off the top of the trailer. A sizable chunk of the thick buildup came straight at Ken, nailing him on the top of his head. He went right down.

"Ken! Are you OK?" Powers saw the impact while looking in his side-view mirror.

"Ken!"

No answer, the young man lay sprawled out on the ground. Ken was out cold.

"911, what is your emergency?"

"I have a man down here at my lot. He is not responding. We need someone here right away, 42 Kelly Road, at the depot. We will have the gate open and someone waiting for the EMS rig. God, please hurry!"

Bill knew the danger of a head injury. This was not a broken leg or arm, which he had seen many times around the yard and in the sorting facility. One of his men, his favorite worker, and a friend, was out cold. He prayed to himself. "God, please let him be OK. He is a young man."

FAVORITE TIME OF YEAR

Ken Heet found himself on an old, splintered bench, his usual spot after a run around the field. This had been his course since elementary school when he began timing himself on mile runs. It was a big field. Four laps equaled one mile. He preferred running here versus the flat, drab track at the high school. He would run there when required. The track was where the team times were recorded, but the field was special. This was the place that gave him an edge on his competition. He put in the extra work. The additional sweat paid dividends. Around the baseball backstop, then along the edge of the woods filled with glowing maples and birch trees, towering white pines, and an occasional mighty oak. It was old-growth wood, not yet cleared for development. The acreage was owned by the school district, with his former school, Rosewood Elementary, sitting on this beautiful land.

Ken knew what time of year it was. He could smell it, feel it, and most dramatically see it. The leaves were in color, peak fall foliage. It was his favorite time of year — heaven, if only for two or three weeks. The smell, that smell of the clean, cool, crisp air. He waited for this all year. Sweatshirt weather. Soon bulky coat time would come, but not yet. This was prime football weather. Early in the season was a bit too hot, and later, playoff time, could be too cold. October, it had to be October. However, last he remembered it was winter, December, and he was heading in for some holiday overtime. How the hell did he end up on his favorite old bench? He hadn't run here in years, many years. Ken had become a treadmill or elliptical-trainer type. Roadwork was in the past.

He heard something loud and recognized the rumble. He turned to see the source and was greeted with another familiar sound. Hard rock music was blasting from what clearly was an aftermarket sound system installed in a Mustang, a red 5.0-liter 'Stang that was tooling around the parking lot behind the field. The car was immaculate. The owner must have had it refurbished to factory specs. Either that or it had been garaged for years, taken out for special occasions, such as a crisp fall day. He knew that song, "Still of the Night" by Whitesnake. Wow, nobody listens to that stuff anymore, and that guy is cranking it. He must be an old-timer, a thirtysomething like Ken, clawing for the old days. He must have some money to keep a ride like that in mint condition.

When Ken stood up from the bench, his six-foot frame felt sturdier, his muscles nimbler. He was surprised, very surprised, when he got a look at the driver and passenger of the Mustang. They weren't older guys; they were kids. Kids with long hair who couldn't have had their licenses very long. They must be wealthy, at least the driver. His parents hooked him up with the coolest of reconditioned or barely used cars. The driver punched the gas and the rear end kicked sideways, veering towards the curb. Typical for that car, light ass end, both tires spinning, lots of power. Ken had seen it before. Lucky the kid he had enough sense to take his foot off the pedal and regain control of that beast. Many others, old and young, hadn't been so smart and tore up those powerful cars. Off the kids and the car went, the music still blaring for all to hear: "Still of the night, still of the night..."

Ken looked down at his feet and noticed something odd, an old pair of Puma sneakers. He hadn't owned a pair of these since high school. He got it now. He was dreaming, which explained the mint 'Stang and the old high school tunes. This would end soon. His dreams never lasted long. Any minute he would snap out of this. He didn't dream much, and when he did, he realized it was just a mirage that would end quickly. Well, if I am dreaming, I should make the most of it and take a walk around on this beautiful day. He remembered the route. He'd taken it since fourth grade when his family moved to the neighborhood. Might as well keep moving until snapping out of it and heading back to his mundane reality.

As he moved along, Ken had the post-run sensation. His legs felt a little burned, but not too bad. He never overdid it. The goal was to build up his lungs. Let your opponents gas out; then you run around them and score. That is the key to the game – and of course teamwork. He got going, strolling to the neighborhood, taking his time. Go slow, be happy. Why rush? He should be waking up soon. Enjoy it.

He cleared the school grounds and headed up Maple Way. Things looked as they always did this time of year. Leaves were raked in piles to the edge of the lawns all along the road. These homeowners took the time to tidy up their piece of America. The village had a vacuum truck that would come along and suck the leaves up, taxpayer dollars at work. The locals loved it: Their money in action.

He made his way up the street and saw some familiar faces raking their lawns, the Davises, the Snides, the Baileys all waved, and he waved back. He had forgotten about these people. Many of the old neighbors had moved out years ago. Some ventured to other states, others to bigger homes, the ones on this block a starter home for many. This was very unusual. He never had such detail in his dreams.

What happened next would take the dream to a new level, a pleasant surprise. Ken looked down the block and saw two of his favorite people in the world coming at him, his grandparents. They walked the neighborhood daily in good weather, but also ventured out in some nasty stuff to keep their blood flowing. His grandfather said that was what kept them healthy. Both appeared spry for their age, with all their working parts in good order. No knee or hip replacements for these two. They lived not far from his parents' home. The families of that time desired closeness, at least Ken's did. He had spent many days and nights at his grandparents' while his folks worked or went out to dinner.

The elder Heets had a look of complete joy as they approached, walking hand in hand as they always did. People did not do that much anymore. Ken wasn't sure why. Perhaps due to the fact they were on their cell phones so much, texting and chatting. His grandparents strolled along as if they were walking on clouds. They always looked that way. He had never seen two people so happy to be together. What was the secret to that? It dawned on him that he had never asked them.

"Kenny, coming back from a run?"

"Yeah, Grandpa, I am, nice day for it."

"Did you time it today?"

"No, no I didn't. I just enjoyed it."

What he really enjoyed was talking to people who had been dead for years. They both would be gone soon. They seemed so healthy. Ken had come along later in the life of his parents. His father's parents were well past retirement age by the time Ken hit high school. When Ken's grandmother died unexpectedly, his grandfather passed away shortly after. Ken figured it was a broken heart. The daily walks had stopped; he no longer had a friend to walk with.

"Kenny, we are heading back. Come on over for something to eat," his grandmother said, stepping into the conversation and adding what she most often did, an offer of food.

"That sounds great."

Ken realized this was his greatest dream. His brain was looking out for him. God, he needed this. He had erred greatly by not asking his grandparents questions when he had the chance. These were the people who lived long, fruitful, loving lives. These were the people with the answers. Most folks never bother to seek advice from them. Aah, youth is so often wasted on the young.

He entered their home, then walked into the living room. It was just as he remembered. The fresh clean smell of the home of two people and one cat. A tidy cat at that, Felix never left the house. The furniture was older, but neat and clean and having limited use. People didn't stop by much anymore.

"Big game coming up, Ken. Tomorrow night is gonna be a good one."

"Your grandfather has had the date circled on the calendar since the day the schedule came out."

"Yeah, big game for sure."

At this point in the dream, Ken felt a bit lost. He may have remembered a lot about the house, the neighborhood, and the school, but he had no idea what opponent his grandparents were talking about.

His grandmother came in with cheese, crackers, and some fruit, always offering a healthy option, and a pitcher of iced tea.

"Well, I think the Eagles are beatable this year. Most of their really good players graduated. This is your year, Ken."

He almost said, "Thank you, Grandpa, you clued me in." The game would be against Little Falls High, the Eagles of the Falls, but there was no way this dream is going that far. Ken was certain he wouldn't make it to the game. He figured this experience would end any moment. Now was the time to ask the questions. He was going to wake up soon.

"Sure, sure, we can beat them."

"You don't sound too up about this game, Ken. Usually you are a ball of fire before a game like this."

True, Grandpa, when I was eighteen, I would have been. But the thirty-three-year-old Ken had caught on to the fact high school games come and go. What he really wanted to do was pick his grandparents' brains, and not about football.

"Oh, I am up. I was out there running on my own time, right? Going beyond what the team had been doing."

"You always do that, Ken. That is what makes you so good."

Now was the time. Spit it out, Ken.

"I have been meaning to ask you two something, and I keep putting it off."

"Oh, oh, he needs money!" This said with a big grandfatherly laugh.

"No, no, not that. I want to ask for advice."

Both grandparents displayed a look of surprise.

"Well, I'll be damned. A younger person wants some advice from us old-timers. What do you say about that, Judy?"

"Doesn't happen every day, that's for sure. We figured you kids had it all figured out." A little sarcasm from one of the sweetest people Ken had ever known.

"OK, Ken, what is it? What would you like to know?"

"You two always seem so happy. I have never seen you down. What is it? What is the secret to that?"

"That's easy, Kenny. Attitude and gratitude; I even made it rhyme for you!" Again with a big laugh.

"He is right, Ken. That's it. You can't take things for granted. If you are healthy and can get around, then it is all good. So many people can't do that. It is not until you get really sick that you realize how important health is. I know for a young person like yourself, that seems simple. You take it for granted."

"Yes, and stay positive, Ken. You have that going for you now, and believe it or not, your dad did too at one time. He was just like you as a young guy, a go-getter, athletic. You look just like him. At least, how he did look."

Ken got along fine with his father. The man had always provided for the family, going to work daily, coming home, tending to the needs of the house and all its inhabitants. He would lay down the law when required, but he was a fair man. He didn't push his son into any particular sport, but offered support once the decision was made. Ken Sr. encouraged his boy to put in the work if he jumped into the game. He expected his son to hustle above and beyond his teammates. Never a chatty man, he had grown more silent each year. He gave the appearance of a beaten soul, going through the motions, on a road to nowhere. In recent years, Ken came to understand his father better, realizing they were quite similar. He hadn't tried to emulate his father. It had just worked out that way. Perhaps it was part of a genetic code, they were wired to be adventurous young men, who cool quickly as they age. His grandfather shared a similar genetic code but was quite the opposite. It must be, as Grandpa Joe said, "All in your attitude."

"He doesn't talk much anymore, Grandpa. Seems to be down in the dumps."

"Kenny, that happens if you let it happen. Will yourself to be more, set small objectives, and keep moving forward. Don't lie down in the road. Like you, he was a hell of an athlete, and when things didn't pan out, he let it get to him. The sports stuff is small potatoes. Very few make anything of it. Have fun, and if you don't get hurt too badly, you are a winner. Set yourself up to win the game of life. I know your grandmother mentioned how I mark your games on the calendar, and get jazzed up, but it is just for fun. It gives us a little something to look forward to. You know I would just as well go to a science fair or the like, if you were into those school clubs." Ken's grandfather knew that wasn't happening. His grandson was no scholar.

"Yes, Ken, and smile. It helps. You will feel better, and the people around you will feel better."

"I noticed that about you and Grandpa, especially when you are out on your walks, always smiling."

"It's contagious. If one of us smiles, so does the other. It helps the soul, lifts you up. It will lighten most any room." Ken's grandmother was smiling ear to ear, and the room was indeed lighter. There was love in that smile and in that room.

"Remember, Kenny, keep things in perspective. You don't have to think small and limit yourself. But be happy for the little things, health and family. Little things add up to big things."

Ken had more questions, important ones. He wanted to get them in when he had the chance. His grandmother stood up and left the room for the moment. It was good timing.

"How did you meet Grandma? What attracted you to her?"

"Well, don't judge a book by its cover. I know you guys, especially you jocks, chase after the really pretty ones, the popular girls. That's fine, but you've got to look beyond that, Ken. You must look inside the person. Let me tell you, the looks, they fade for all of us. I have seen it my whole life. But a good soul, that lasts forever. Look into a person's eyes and see their smile. It can tell you a lot. It is a glimpse into their soul."

Perhaps this was a dig at Stacy, who would have been Ken's girl at the time. His grandfather met her and had likely sized up her personality. Ken sat silently after that, taking it in.

"Sometimes you know, you can just tell the good ones, but you hesitate, for whatever reason, and someone else snatches them up. Gone forever, Ken, off with some other guy, who could be a jerk. But he made his move, and you're standing there holding feathers."

"So if I see a girl that seems like a good person, I should say something, don't just stand there."

"That's what I'm saying, Kenny, that's it. You can stay for dinner if you want, pot roast tonight."

As much as Ken loved his grandparents, he vividly recalled the pot roast.

"Not tonight. But thanks for the invitation, and more importantly thank you for the advice. With all the wisdom you two have, I feel foolish for not asking for more advice over the years."

His grandmother walked in and heard Ken's comment.

"We love the fact you are asking for advice. Nobody asks us, Ken. We are old news!"

"That's a big mistake, Grandma, a huge one."

This was a man in his thirties in his eighteen-year-old body taking an opportunity he had missed many years ago.

"I will add a little bit to what your grandfather said. Life comes down to decisions. We all make some bad ones, but overall you want to keep moving forward. The decisions you make will determine how far you go. You will learn this over the years. The stuff a kid learns in math or science class is interesting, but life is the greatest teacher of all. You will pick it up over the years."

She encapsulated a lot in that one short statement. His grandmother had it down and moved through life with a quiet purpose.

"We are always here, Ken. Anytime you need advice, or anything at all, stop by or call."

Ken was happy he had asked the questions right then and there. As healthy as his grandparents appeared, it wouldn't be long until both were gone from this world.

"Thanks, Grandma, thanks for all that you two have done for me over the years."

Ken had heard similar advice over time and would continue to hear it as he aged. Listening and hearing are two different things. It was well past time to take in what was being given for free.

His grandfather found his grandson's question and overall demeanor odd. This wasn't carefree Kenny sitting in his living room.

"Are you OK, Kenny? Everything all right?"

"Sure, I'm fine. Just been thinking a lot lately. I have to get going. I need to sack out early tonight."

"We will be at the game tomorrow, first ones there. We'll get the good seats."

"Goodnight and thanks again. I think we will play well. I'm feeling good."

Ken headed home. The long, strange dream was rolling on, but it had to end soon. He would snap out of this in a flash, he was sure, but he was taking some great advice with him.

"Joe, you thinking what I'm thinking?"

"Yeah, he must have a crush on a new girl."

* * *

Ken knew the route to his parents' home so well, he could have done it blindfolded. As he made his way darkness was settling, creeping in early in the fall. He would take this dream for all it was worth, although he began to wonder if he was stuck here? Perhaps he had died. Is this what happens when you crap out? If so, he decided, this is pretty good. Might as well play it out.

"Ken, where have you been? Dinner has been ready for a while."

He could smell his favorite dish, his mother's masterpiece, chicken and dumplings. This wasn't Grandma's pot roast, thank goodness. This was the good stuff. Mom was taking care of him the night before the big game.

"Sorry, I stopped by to talk with Grandma and Grandpa. I ran into them after laps at the school."

"That's nice that you stopped in. You don't get over there much anymore. I am sure they loved to see you."

"Oh yeah, it was great. They will be there tomorrow night. They were pumped."

Ken's mother looked just as he had remembered during his school days. Janice Heet was a pretty woman who had married her high school boyfriend and had led a conventional life taking care of her small family.

She never complained about any material items they may have lacked. It was a quiet, content household. His parents moved out of the state just after Ken started working at the parcel depot. Ken Sr. had talked about it for years and finally got up the gumption to do it. Their son rarely saw them after that.

"Your father already ate. He is watching TV if you want to take your plate in and eat in the living room."

"I think I'll sit here with you. The chicken smells awesome."

Given the option, her son usually took the TV room. Janice couldn't help but wonder if something was up.

"All right, the plate is on the counter."

"Thanks. We can talk."

Now she was really surprised but was happy to sit with her son.

"Ken, is something up?"

"No, no, just don't get a chance to talk much."

They each took a seat at the table. The chicken and dumplings were still warm.

"You excited about tomorrow night?

"Sure, sure I am. I think we will do well." His nonchalant answer puzzled his mother.

"Well, you sound pretty relaxed. I guess that is a good thing. I remember your father jumping out of his shoes before the big games. You would have thought he was being paid to play."

"It is a game Mom, just a game. If we win, awesome. If nobody gets hurt, that's even more awesome."

Janice now thought someone had kidnapped her son and sent in an imposter. But she liked it. No, she loved it. She knew all too well what happens when people put way too much emphasis on sports and lose sight of the big picture.

"Ken, that is the wisest thing I have heard you say. You are right. If nobody gets hurt, it is all good."

"How is Dad today?"

That was a rhetorical question since Ken Sr. was the same every day, no crazy highs or lows. The man was just there, putting one foot in front of the other making his way through life.

"He seems fine, like always. He will head over there with your grandparents tomorrow, an early show-up. I will be helping in the concession stand, so I will be early also."

Ken entered the living room and found his dad just as he had remembered him. He was sitting in his recliner, legs up, watching the end of the evening news. It was a routine. He didn't talk much about national events, but he did watch the network news to keep abreast of what was going on in the Cold War. Things had been cooling with a new man in charge in the U.S.S.R. Long-term reconciliation of some kind seemed possible. This was an issue even the casual observer of international affairs took note of.

"Hi Dad, what's up?"

"Hello Ken, same old. Just watching the news. Looks like we may have a thaw in the Cold War, good news."

Oh yes, Dad, you will see that all right. Not too long down the road the whole house of cards will fall for the Soviets. His father would find out soon enough.

Ken was often told how much he looked like Ken Sr. In high school photos of his dad, the resemblance was even more obvious. Both had dark hair, brown eyes, and an athletic build with similar physical proportions. Ken now realized they had aged the same. They were holding up well but underwhelmed about what life offered.

"Ready for the game tomorrow?"

"Yeah, everyone seems pretty hyped up about it."

"You're not?"

"Oh sure, sure I am. It is another game, Dad. It will be good. It's all good. I will try to have fun with it. You know, sit back and enjoy it for what it is worth."

Ken Sr. was taken aback. His son, usually jovial about the big games, was relaxed. His father loved it. What had taken a long time to sink in for the father, had come early for his son. It is just a game; enjoy it.

"Ken, you got it, you really have it. Hold onto that thought. It is a good one."

Ken and his dad engaged in small talk, nice, casual conversation. He didn't quiz his father on any concerns about life, as he had his grandparents. He was enjoying warm words with a man he hadn't talked with enough when growing up. His father was always there for him. He respected his father and appreciated him and was happy that he valued his son's new take on the sports world. It was a pleasant feeling.

"Dad, I am hitting the sack early tonight, big day tomorrow."

"Yeah, sure, get some rest. I won't see you till the game. I'm heading into work early."

"See you tomorrow, Dad. It should be a good one."

* * *

His room was just as remembered, small, but tidy. His mother wasn't one to baby her son, but she did make sure the room was kept clean, even if she had to do it. His old, weathered book bag, a hand-me-down from his father, was at the small desk near the one window in the room. As usual, the bag was closed, with the books staying inside while it was in his room. He had a sports study hall and was able to complete most of his assignments during that period. Ken did not carry a taxing course load, taking what was required. That was enough for him and the athletic department. His parents would have liked a little more, but they never received any negative feedback from any member of the school staff. Just the opposite, most teachers liked their son, a jock who tried to do his best.

Ken took a seat at the small desk and unzipped the bag. He didn't recall all the classes he had taken as a senior. Curiosity was calling. The first binder he pulled out was labeled "Health Class." He definitely remembered that one. It was taught by George King, the head football coach, who also handled some gym classes for the main student body. The coach was universally liked by students and staff. Even the punky kids appreciated him. He was never demeaning to anyone and had a commanding presence that let you know he was a serious but fair man. Not particularly big framed, he stayed in excellent physical shape. Ken wasn't sure how old Coach King was, but he certainly looked younger than his age. He displayed empathy, always trying to make the students he dealt with feel better about themselves. He emphasized improvement by increments; small steps lead to big gains if you keep at it. The coach never sent any flack towards the nonathletic kids. He encouraged them to do the best they could. He believed people are just looking for respect and a little bit of it can go a long way. If anyone was treated a bit tougher, it was his athletes. But they expected it and were used to it.

The coach may have been super fit, but he died young. Five years after graduation, Ken attended the great man's memorial service. He recalled the throngs of people who attended and grieved. A car accident took the life of George King. A drunk driver did him in. Ken rarely cried, and certainly not in public, but that day he could not hold back. He and scores of others were reduced to puddles of tears.

A note was attached to the front of the health class folder "presentation Friday, October 10th." The small calendar on his desk had the days crossed off until the 10th, with "Eagles" written on that Friday. It was tomorrow, the big game and a presentation on the same day. Ken opened the binder and saw on lined composition paper the title "How physical conditioning affects your mental well-being." This was typical of the topics Coach King emphasized and definitely a softball for Ken. He read some notes in his own handwriting penned on the sheet. The notes addressed perfusion, detailing how the heart spreads blood and oxygen through the body, removing carbon dioxide so that fresh, oxygenated blood is sent back to the organs. Ken had always been fascinated by that process, which is why he nabbed the topic for his presentation. He had a vague memory of giving a speech about it but could not recall the exact format. No bother, when the time this speech came around, he'd have snapped out of this dream and got back to reality.

If he didn't snap out by then, something clearly was happening. If he were to lie down on the bed behind him, fall asleep, and wake up tomorrow for a day at school and the big game, then no way was this a typical dream. It had to be something totally different. His fascination with time travel might have taken him exactly where he had longed to be. The question then would be, "Do I really want to be here?" He closed the binder, put it back in the bag, and lay down in the small bed he had slept in since he was child. His heart rate bumped up a bit. It is scary to get what you wish for.

He might still be here tomorrow. The game wasn't his number one concern. He had a bigger task. Ken would have to take on a public speaking spot, something he never enjoyed. Running towards the end zone came naturally. Standing in front of a group and giving a speech was not in his wheelhouse. But this was a promising scenario. Ken now had many years of knowledge behind him. He was much more familiar with the ways of the world than the teenagers who would compose the audience. He had the chance to give them an earful. What an opportunity.

BACK TO SCHOOL

Ken awoke and knew instantly he was still in his old room. He had to be. His tall frame crammed like a sardine into the tiny mattress of his youth. When he got his first apartment, after getting his first real job, the first thing on the list was a full-size mattress. He liked to spread out. Now things were getting really interesting. This was no dream, he was back in time, or he was dead. It had all happened so quickly. What to do? After mulling it over for a minute he came to a conclusion: there was nothing he could do. Might as well enjoy it. He had wished for this for some time. What could he do? Run downstairs and say, "Mom, I am back from the future…" She would have the mental health hotline on the phone in minutes and call his father home from work.

So, there he was, with what most would feel is a golden opportunity. He had the chance to do it all over again, now with the knowledge of the future at hand. Hey, just think of the stock picks he could make or the bets he could place on ball games. Maybe so, but right now he had an immediate concern; he had a speech to give.

"Ken, are you up? You better get moving." His mother was calling. Things had not changed. He often lumbered in bed too long, just making it to class before the bell.

"I'm up. I'll be down."

He popped out of bed and got in the shower. It was like he had never left the house. He lived there for many years. They had moved in when he was four years old. It was habitual, pure routine. When done in the bathroom, he cracked open the dresser drawer and pulled out his favorite pair of Levi's, nicely broken in and comfy. These jeans weren't the new, stiff ones that he might have worn in a previous school year. These bad boys felt like a layer of tough skin, smooth yet firm. He had the speech coming up, so he looked for a neater shirt than usual, no T-shirt today. He found a nice polo shirt. Might as well go all out. Typically, team members wore their game jersey on the day of the game, but today he would skip that. The coach would understand. He was giving the presentation in his class. Also, on his first day back after so many years, it would be nice to blend in wearing a polo shirt. Looking into the closet, he fished out a cool pair of blue suede Adidas sneakers. He grabbed his book bag and the all-important health-class folder. He was ready to hit the road.

"You have ten minutes to get there, Ken."

"Got it, right on schedule."

Down the stairs, to the fridge, snaring a juice, Ken was in motion. He topped breakfast off with a banana and a snack bar to eat on the way and was out the door in seconds flat. As he moved along, Ken was putting some thought into the speech. He would use the outline he had sketched out on the notepaper, but no doubt this would be mostly ad-lib. Ken had a story to tell. These kids would get an earful in the ten minutes Coach King had allotted.

Ken lived close to school. No need to drive. He had occasionally caught a ride with one of his friends, particularly during foul weather, but today was beautiful. Also, if he had caught a lift, his friends would start asking questions about events he had no clue about. His memory was decent, but not that good. They would be yapping about old gossip, stuff he had moved on from so many years ago.

As he trotted up to Colonial High, he came upon the smoking area first. He had forgotten how many kids smoked back then. The school even had an assigned space for it. He doubted that was the case today, but he wouldn't know. Ken didn't go anywhere near that school after graduation. He tried to move on after walking across the stage.

The next Deja vu sensation was a replica of the experience he had yesterday with the Mustang

GT, only amplified. Now there were a dozen cars rolling in blaring, Motley Crue, Van Halen, and of course Metallica, piping out of sound systems that cost more than the cars they had been installed in. This was most definitely the '80s, an era defined by loud music and big hair. He noted flowing manes on males and females and the smell of hair spray. Ken's hair was moderate, not too long, not too short. Even in high school he was a practical guy. He had a graduating class of about five hundred, so he found himself wading into a sea of teenagers. What surprised him was how few he recognized. He should have taken time to meet more people back in the day, not just the athletes. Variety is good – another lesson he had learned in the years since.

The first person he ran into was not a student. It was Coach King who looked exactly like Ken remembered. The man was standing before him, frozen in time.

"Ken, you are first up today. Don't screw up. I want you to set the tone for the rest of the class."

"I got it, Coach. I have been thinking about it all night."

"All night? I hope you put some work into it before last night."

"Yeah, yes I did, but I was just polishing off the thoughts."

"You will do well, Ken. How do you feel about tonight?"

"Great, 100 percent. We've got this, Coach."

"That is exactly what I wanted to hear. See you in a bit."

Off he went, one of the best guys Ken had ever known. Should he tell him? How would he say it? "Coach, not too long from now you will be killed in a car wreck." What would King do, not drive? Ken could not recall the date of the accident. The warning would not be specific. And then of course there was the grandfather paradox, which David Sphere talked about. Does he really want to monkey around with past events? Although in this case, he was sure it would trigger a positive chain reaction since nothing good came out of Coach King dying young. Ken realized again that if he broached these topics with anyone, coach included, they would immediately think he was crazy or on drugs. It was an odd spot to be in. He was back where he wanted to be but could not do anything about what he knew was going to happen. That was the paradox.

The next friendly face was Stacy Randall, a girl he had dated for a few months. That would end when she went away to college. Stacy was smart and pretty, but Ken figured he wasn't what she had in mind for anything long-term. Stacy was going places, and Ken would not be there with her. Such is life.

"Hey stranger, haven't heard from you in a bit."

Ken wanted to say, "Naturally you haven't. I have been many years away from you tooling around in a rig in a dismal parking lot." Those words were best kept to himself.

"Yeah, I am really sorry, been busy, I have a presentation in a little bit and the game later."

"Oh yeah, should be a real big crowd. You guys have some great weather for it. Lucky this game wasn't later in the season."

Stacy wasn't a huge sports fan, but she tried. She and Ken didn't have that much in common. They were set up by friends, and they both knew this wasn't for the long haul. They were just spending some time together.

Ken wanted to say something thoughtful now. He didn't do that enough in the old days, tending to keep things to himself. He had learned a kind word, or words, can make a difference in a person's life. No sense holding the sentiment inside.

"Stacy, you look great today. I mean you always look good, but today even better. The outfit is dynamite."

He felt she would appreciate that. Stacy was a girl who took particular care of her appearance. She took pride in how she presented herself. Nothing wrong with that, not for everyone, but she wore it well. She put time and effort into it. He might as well acknowledge it. It was the polite thing to do.

"Thank you, Kenny. I just got this last week. Got a decent deal on it too."

The first bell rang, a warning to get moving. A quick kiss and Stacy was on her way. Ken wasn't sure what became of her, but he had heard she had moved away. She was one who preferred a warmer climate and mentioned it often. Such moves were common in this community, with most folks never returning. He was never a hot-weather guy. Here is where he would stay. For good or bad, this would be home.

He walked down the hall to the lower level and the science wing where the health class was located. He remembered because it was close to the weight room and the gym. Ken had spent a great deal of his school days in that area of the school. It looked exactly as he had remembered.

"Kenny, ready to go, buddy?"

It was Mike Cardin, a solid guy and good team-mate who sat across from him in class. He too would have a turn at the mini-presentation, but Ken would go first, the way Coach King wanted it.

"I think I will do all right. I laid out an outline and will riff a bit. Don't be afraid to ask questions if I finish too quickly and get stuck up there. Kill the clock!"

"No problem, and what about tonight? You think we got it?"

"We got it. Might be tight, but we got it."

"Confidence, I like it, Ken. I agree, we will do it."

Mike would turn out to be a success story, doing very well for himself as the years rolled on. Ken often saw his old friend's advertisements. Mike was local and stayed local, operating an investment office. He was honest, and honesty plays well in that line of work. Finances are at the top of concerns for people from all walks of life. Mike settled the minds of many. He had a long list of happy customers. Mike chose a profession that suited him well.

Ken and his buddy filed in with the rest of the class, twenty or so in total, typical for his school. Everyone was present today, and now he recognized some faces. Kids he had in other classes, a few going back to grammar school. Most of them were good people. He was fortunate. There weren't too many knuckleheads in the school. There wasn't the level of drama one might see across the country nowadays. Sure, they had problems back then, but nothing monumental. It was a different time for sure.

He reached into his backpack and pulled out the health class folder and skimmed over his notations. No need to get nervous. That only makes things worse. He was among friends, a well-liked kid at the school. These simpler times were nice. He could get used to this. Hell, he may have to get used to it. For all he knew he was trapped in the past and would have to live these days over. Time will tell, so they say. No choice but to sit back and take it in.

Coach King entered the classroom. Time to get the show on the road. Not one to vary from a schedule, time management being a big part of the man's life. On the field or in the class, they were on the clock.

"All right people, we all know what starts today, and you should all know the order that you are going in. We will see how many we can get through. As I said, ten minutes, but I am not going to give you the hook if you are doing a good job and we have class participation. Everyone can learn a lot here. These are topics that can help you in life. I don't care what you do, this material can benefit all of us in this room."

The topics revolved around physical and mental health and how, to a large extent, we have control of physical and mental well-being. Certainly not always, but to a large degree it is possible for people to set themselves up for fruitful lives. That was the take on things from the standpoint of George King. Ken had heard it in the locker room, on the practice field, on the playing field, and now in the classroom. It was a great message.

King shifted his gaze toward Ken Heet signaling it was time. It was the same look he had seen at practice and during a game. It was King's "Don't screw this up look." Ken was familiar with it, and he did what he always did when King gave him the look. He smiled. Get ready for this, Coach. You and the kids are about to get an earful. You are going to see and hear a different version of Ken Heet.

THE SPEECH

Ken, with his single sheet of note paper, made his way to the lectern. He liked the idea of having a structure to lean on for this presentation. There were times when he preferred to move around the room and not be tied to the wood podium located stage right. Not today. This was preaching time. The lectern would work well. He didn't want to take on the persona of a reverend, proselytizing to a group of high school students. It wouldn't play well in this room. His plan was to keep it simple. That was his general view on life; don't complicate things. Normally he would be nervous taking on a solo speaking role. Not this time. He hadn't practiced, other than running thoughts through his head and jotting down notes. Ken had his grandparents in his corner. They unknowingly had prepared him for this moment. What they said during the chat the day before had great meaning. He was about to channel their thoughts into the class of twenty students and one coach. Ken was in a unique position. At the lectern stood an eighteen-year-old body with the mind of a man approaching middle age. He was about to unload a seasoned view on a group that viewed him as a peer. Hopefully, they would take the advice to heart.

He paused and looked around the class. Some faces he recognized, most he did not, it had been a long time. A girl sitting near the front caught his attention. She had kind, calm eyes, and as Grandpa Joe had said, the eyes are a glimpse into the soul. She presented herself as a composed young woman. He vaguely remembered her, and if his recollection was correct, she was smart. A student like her was tracked with the brighter kids. Ken would not have been in many, if any, other classes with her. Health class was a catch-all. All levels of students were here, a required course for everybody.

"Good morning, everyone. For those of you who don't know me, I'm Ken Heet."

Great, off to an odd start. Of course they know who you are. You are their classmate and the resident alpha jock, the teacher's pet. They don't know you took a trip in time to be here today. Relax, Kenny, this is just a group of kids. He looked down at his notes: "How physical conditioning affects your mental well-being." Good place to start. Tell them what you plan to talk about.

"Today I will talk about the importance of physical conditioning and how it relates to a person's mental health. If you feel good physically, you are more likely to have a positive outlook on life. It makes perfect sense. To feel good physically there is no need to compete against others. You don't have to run a five-minute mile or bench press three hundred pounds to feel good physically. What is important is doing what you are capable of doing and aiming for improvement. Even staying level is helpful. No need to claw for gains if that isn't for you. Just keeping your heart rate up for set periods could be good enough. Whatever it is that makes you feel good, makes you feel alive, if it is legal of course."

He was keeping it light, and the last line got some laughter. A more serious tone would follow. Kenny Heet was easing into his presentation. Coach King was taking notice. He knew the topic his star athlete had chosen, no surprise there. What was unexpected was the tone being set. The coach thought Ken would start off with bravado, with words about how you must test yourself, set ambitious goals, strive to be the best. That was the Ken he knew. The kid who, on and off-season, put in more work than any other player on the team. Now what King was hearing was a mellowed mindset. This wasn't a testosterone-filled start to a presentation. The kid sounded mature.

Ken looked down at his notes again and noted point number two: Perfusion. This was one of the required parts of the presentation. He would incorporate some elements that had been discussed in some detail during class. But of course, that was a long time ago. Good thing he had notes. After he covered this part, the freewheeling would begin and off script he would go.

"We have talked about perfusion in this class, and I found it really interesting. I will be the first to admit, I am not a strong science student. Or anatomy, or really any academic subject to be quite honest." This drew some chuckles. The pretty girl sitting to his left got a kick out of it. She knew Ken was not an academic.

"I never like it when people read verbatim definitions when giving presentations. It puts people to sleep. But I am going to do it just once for my block." He looked down at his notes and read the definition as taken from the issued textbook.

> "The supply of oxygen and removal of wastes from the body's cells and tissues as the result of the flow of blood through the capillaries. If for some reason the blood is not adequately circulated, the organs may not receive adequate supplies of oxygen and dangerous waste products build up, which can lead to hypo perfusion also known as shock."

"There, that is it, perfusion. I promise I won't read to you again. Obviously, shock is a worst-case scenario, likely tied to some sort of injury. But there we have it, the circulatory system. The heart, blood, and blood vessels. That keeps us going, or perfused. Also, there are the lungs which get the O2 into the blood, but I don't want to get too far off course. The more technical I get, the more likely I am to say something incorrect and embarrass myself. I will stop while I'm ahead."

More laughs at the levity of Ken the jock.

"So, what does that all mean? To me it means the better the blood flows, the healthier our bodies. Our skin, brain, heart, and all our organs rely on perfusion. Prior to this class I didn't think a lot about that. I figured you breathe in air, it goes to your lungs, and you keep moving along, one foot in front of the other. Yet there is more to it. I realize I should have picked this up in biology, but like I said, studiousness has never been my specialty. I am picking things up now because Coach King is teaching, and the man intimidates me."

Again, more laughter. This time, beyond light chuckles. Ken was holding their attention and ready to move into the meat of his presentation.

"How do we do it? How do we keep perfused, and in doing so improve our health and mental state? Forget about the intense workouts on the track, treadmill, or in the weight room. We have the perfect opportunity right at our doorstep. For all the complaining about the weather around here, we have wide open beauty right in front of us, especially this time of year. It's free, no membership charge. Head out for a hike. I tell you when you get to the top you can see a piece of heaven. You don't even have to go to the high peaks, go to the small ones, the easy trails. Open your eyes, take it in, breathe the air. With the colors of the leaves, you will feel like you are looking at a painting. Man, I tell you, if you don't get a positive vibe from that, you must be brain dead. You see, you are combining physical and mental enrichment into one activity. It isn't like football where someone is trying to take your head off, which is a much tougher way to get your perfusion going."

The laughs kept coming. The kid in front of the room was making light of the sport that they all assumed he lived for. Coach King loved it. Ken was growing up. It was now time for the heart of the matter. Now the thoughts of a mind with thirty-plus years on Earth will come out of the teen body at the podium. The kids might put more stock in what he was about to say. He was one of them, not an old-timer.

"I saw two people walking down the street hand in hand last night who looked like they won the lottery, won millions. But they hadn't. It looked like they were walking on clouds, big smiles on their faces. They weren't two young lovebirds; they were my grandparents."

The room got quiet as Ken softened his voice. He wasn't kidding now. He was speaking from the heart.

"You can't buy that, not for any amount of money. That is the best type of exercise, a simple walk that will build your body, mind, and heart. Without a doubt that is the combination of physical and mental health, and once again, it doesn't cost a dime. How much longer do you think people live if they walk like that? Not just the number of years, but good years, quality time. Nobody lives forever. We have a limited time on the planet. We don't know what will happen. I know we are eighteen or so and don't put much thought into things like that, but we should. I think as we grow older, we will realize it is all fleeting and time waits for no one."

As Ken said this, he looked over at Coach King who would be dead not too long from that moment. A great man's life cut short. King looked back at his student and star athlete and had no idea where this was coming from. What the hell got into Kenny Heet?

"Without the activity, without something to look forward to, people start to wander, and in come the negative thoughts. Those thoughts can eat away at your insides, your soul. It is hard to be negative when sitting on top of a mountain you just climbed, hard not to smile when you are walking down the street with someone you have spent the last forty years with. If you don't have a person to walk with, get a dog to keep you company. You and your canine friend will enjoy the exercise and mental strength that comes with it. Don't forget about mutts. They need love too, no need for an expensive pet."

He noted the girl, front left, had a big smile after he said that. Someone was taking note.

"You have it right in front of you. You can't lose, a low-cost or no-cost option to feed your body, brain, and soul. Don't sit on the fence and watch the world go by because before you know it, it will indeed have passed by. You will have missed the bus. It is the little things that can make the greatest difference in the quality of your life, and certainly your physical and mental well-being. I think most everyone in this room knows what the good choices are. Be sure to make them. Avoid the bad choices, the ones that come back to bite you. Often you know at the time it isn't a good move, but people follow the flock, right over the edge. Life isn't always so hard. We sometimes make it that way ourselves by making dumb decisions. Keep it simple and live well."

Ken figured he had made his point, no need to beat it into the ground. He wasn't sure how well received his message was. He got it out and it felt good. Time to wrap it up.

"Well anyway, in conclusion, poor perfusion, or malperfusion as the book says, causes health problems. Cardiovascular disease, coronary artery disease, and other conditions as listed in the text, but like I said, I don't want to read to you verbatim. I just want to emphasize the importance of getting out there and getting after something you enjoy doing. We have a lot to do right in front of us, especially this time of year. Get out and get some. Lastly, remember this: If you have your health, you have everything. Pretty appropriate closing for a health class presentation I would say. Are there any questions?"

Nobody raised a hand or said a word, an eerie quiet came over the room.

"In that case, thank you for your time. I hope you picked something from this. Thank you for listening."

Ken stepped away from the podium feeling good about what he said. It was simple advice, but he had found life to be as simple as you make it. He had used less than the allotted ten minutes, having left time for questions that did not come. The kids in the class were quietly mulling over the words of their classmate.

Ken figured the length of his presentation was about right. When speakers go too long, the audience drifts off; at least that was his experience. He had included the relevant academic information to fulfill class requirements. Overall, not a bad job. The hiking reference had been picked up when dating Susan Lyons. They had dated for a few months not long after graduation, and she was the one who had gotten him into the beauty of the outdoors. He had no idea what became of her. She left the area after college, heading south. He was sure she was doing well. Her attitude surely carried her to good places. Susan was just another of many people who had passed through his life, gone but not forgotten. He thought he should take some of his own advice and get up to the mountaintops again. It had been a while. A little less overtime, and more Kenny time was in order. Practice what you preach.

Coach King stood up and headed to the front of the class to move things along.

"Thank you, Ken. That was a nice job. We learned a great deal not only about perfusion and circulation, but we also got some sound advice about life, and that's why we are here."

The room was quiet. No one was sure what to make out of the newly pensive Kenny Heet.

"OK, next up is Karen Davis, who will address the topic of diet and bone density."

Good luck, Karen, you have to follow Ken and wax on about the importance of calcium in one's diet.

After a few more mundane presentations, far less poignant than Ken's, the class was over. The kids began to filter out. Most shot a smile at the jock who turned out to be much more thoughtful than anyone had anticipated. The most surprised was George King, who pulled his running back aside.

"Where the heck did that come from, Ken? Did you hit your head on something? I thought I might have had a Ken Heet imposter up there."

King was smiling, clearly he was impressed. He liked what he heard.

"It came from the heart. Sometimes you have to reach down and say what you feel, what you think should be said, versus what people want to hear."

"Is someone falling in love? You have a crush on a new girl?" King smiled as he said this, but he was only half kidding. Something had happened to Ken Heet, and his coach wasn't sure. Somebody had grown up overnight. He liked it, but he hoped this new sensitivity would not affect his go-to man's playing style. The Heet was needed to win.

"Nah, not at the moment. It was like I said, I ran into my grandparents and actually took some time to talk with them for a bit. I opened my mind a bit."

"Well, it sounded great. You made the others sound like kids up there. I liked it, but I need you to bring it tonight, Kenny. Leave the nice guy on the sidelines." King winked.

"Don't worry. I'm ready to go."

Ken knew something about the game his coach didn't. They were going to win this one. A tough game, but a win was coming. He again thought about warning George King about the car wreck coming his way but couldn't think of how to put it to his coach and mentor. It was best that way. Ken was not here to alter history. That was a wormhole he didn't want to go down.

THE STUDENT LOUNGE

Ken looked at his schedule. American studies was up next. It could be interesting, especially if the class discussed how current events could affect their future. Ken could sit looking like the cat that ate the canary. He might have definitive answers to the speculation, but those would be kept to himself.

As expected, the talk in Mr. Thompson's class that day centered on current events. A new man in charge of the Kremlin was pushing the Soviet Union in a different direction with his policies of glasnost and perestroika. Mikhail Gorbachev was aware that the closed society of the U.S.S.R. was not sustainable. The West was pulling away. The Soviet system could not keep up. Mr. Thompson led the discussion, and all agreed these were very positive developments. Nuclear holocaust seemed less likely. However, the teacher and his students could not imagine that the system, the entire U.S.S.R, would be a thing of the past in the very near future. Ken knew they would be surprised but kept his thoughts to himself. Global change would come calling soon.

Next, he was slated for a forty-five-minute study block. Time to head to the student lounge, a senior-heavy hangout. That had always been a favored spot for Ken and company. He wondered how many people he would recognize. Ken kept a tight set of friends back then, and as he got older the circle became even smaller.

As he entered the lounge, he heard '80s music again, this time piping more quietly from the speakers on the wall. They didn't crank it up in the lounge. This time the tune was a Night Ranger classic, "Sentimental Street," a mellow side of the decade's sound. He hadn't heard the song in many years.

Some of the kids were eating rectangular warmed-up frozen pizza that was popular back then. He wondered if they still served them in the cafeterias of the new millennium.

He didn't see many familiar faces in the crowd as he scanned the room, but he immediately recognized one. There sat the pretty girl from health class. He still could not remember where he knew her from. She was sitting alone in a booth with a textbook open, jotting down notes. He didn't want to bother her, interrupting study time, but he might not get another chance. He was cut a break when she looked up and flashed a smile. Ken recalled the awkward feeling of first approaches, but his feet got moving. It was now or never.

"Hello, I'm Ken. We are in the same class with Coach King."

The pretty eyes warmed. She seemed receptive.

"That was such a nice speech you gave. I felt bad for the people who went after you. Nobody was listening to them, not much anyway. Everyone was thinking about what you said."

"Yeah, I was riffing for the most part. The perfusion stuff I had written down. After that I was just free flowing, blabbing really."

"I really like the part about your grandparents. That was so sweet."

"All true. That just happened, last night. Right time, right place, with the presentation coming up. Do you mind if I sit down?"

That was it. He had made the move. No long casual conversation. He would slide into her personal space if she would let him.

"Sure, sit down."

She pulled in the notepad and book, giving Ken some room. She looked even more attractive. No puffed-up hair or Aqua Net for this girl. This was a practical person. His first impression was sincerity. She was no phony, and not a follower of the crowd.

"I recognize you from somewhere, but I am embarrassed to say I don't know your name."

"Jane, my name is Jane Warner. You probably recognize me from study hall. Last year we had a study hall together."

Looking at the books in her pile, Ken realized his assumption about her academic level was correct. These weren't the textbooks Ken would have been issued. Jane was Advanced Placement material.

"That makes sense. By the looks of things I wouldn't be in any regular class with you." He gave a sheepish look as he read the titles of her textbooks.

"No, other than study hall, I don't recall seeing you in any class. I do know you play football. I have seen your name in the papers."

Nice, she is acknowledging awareness of "The Heet." At least he has that going for him, and he had just displayed the ability to put a rational thought together. She appreciated the speech and must realize he isn't a total dullard.

"Yeah, we have a game tonight. Should be a good one. Are you going?"

Playing with the past be damned, it couldn't hurt to encourage her to attend a game. But what if something happened to her on the way or at the game? Was he playing with history? The hell with it. He was going to attempt a change with this one thing.

"I hadn't planned to go, I had some work to do, but..."

"Come on. Jane, all work no play. You heard my speech. You should get out and have some fun." He smiled.

"I get it though. If you are busy, I understand. Football or sports in general aren't for everyone. I will say the crowds tend to be decent at our games. Not too many loudmouths. The weather is supposed to be nice, a beautiful fall night. Jane, I tell you, this time of year, I just love it. Not just the football stuff. It is the fresh air, leaves floating, the color in the trees. It is really something special. Of course, it only lasts two or three weeks, and then we are bundled up like mummies."

They both laughed, with Ken's assessment being spot on. In a few weeks the heat in the cars would be cranked up, and everyone would be scraping ice and snow off their windshields and sidewalks. Such is life in the Northeast.

"That does sound nice, Ken. Maybe I will come."

"Great, I will arrange for a special seat for you." He gave her a big smile. "Seriously though, students are free. It won't cost anything unless you want some hot chocolate or something. Also, you don't have to sit in the student section. Actually, I would not recommend it. Things tend to be loud there with the bullhorns and all that. Sit with the parents, the families. They are more chill."

"OK, Ken, but I may sit with the students. I

don't want to appear antisocial." Her warm smile continued.

"Fair enough. Seriously, it should be a fun game to watch. The team we are playing is good. They always are. I will be looking for you in the stands. Please don't stand me up." He winked.

The period was winding down. He surmised Jane was not the type to be late for class. For the most part, he was the same way. Far from an obnoxious jock, manners mattered to Ken Heet.

"I have to get going, Ken. I have chemistry class now."

"Ouch, that was a hard one for me, all those tables to remember. I had to take the scaled-down class. They have to spoon-feed that stuff to guys like me."

"Yeah, it can be tricky."

"See you tonight, Jane."

"Sure. It sounds like fun."

Off she went, certainly to be one of the first to take a seat in class. Ken would get moving soon, but he sat for a bit, digesting what had just taken place. He was a strong believer in first impressions and was impressed with Jane Warner. She was much more than a diligent student. A warm, sincere person had been sitting across from him, he was sure of that. His instincts were correct.

Jane's parents were professionals, engineers, who met and married late in life. Their only child was raised in a calm, loving environment. The Warner household was not filled with spontaneity. Activities were planned out in their tidy, orderly home. Lawrence and Diane Warner doted on their daughter, encouraging her to excel at academics as they had. Quiet and bookish by nature, they didn't push Jane into social or athletic activities. They surmised their daughter would find her way in the world, developing her own circle of friends. Jane's parents' primary goal was to ensure their daughter had the skills to succeed in the workforce. Their efforts would prove successful, but their daughter would have a hole in her world. She would move through life alone.

Ken figured he wasn't messing with history too much. He only invited a girl to a football game. He didn't ask her out on a date. Hundreds of kids would be at that game. As he sat in the small booth in the lounge he thought about the passage of time. It is relative. When he was a student, time seemed to move slowly. It could be a struggle getting through long practices, boring school subjects, and catty social situations common in any school setting. But after he was out of school and into his work routine, time began to move quickly. Sure, some nights at the depot dragged on, but the years went by fast. Before he knew it, he was thirty years of age and climbing. When he was a student, thirty seemed old. He had gotten there in no time. The clock wasn't slowing down. The question was what to do after this? If he lingered in the '80s, he would have to make some decisions. How long was this going to last? Was he reliving his life all over or just visiting? Things were getting complicated.

First things first, he had to get through this game. One thing at a time.

THE GAME

Ken was able to navigate the rest of the school day without issue, just like riding a bike. He continued to take in the sights and sounds of the '80s, running into a few teammates, all of whom were stoked about the game. In the main lobby Ken saw a sight that was beginning to disappear from the time he traveled from. A bank of phones lined the wall. A few kids were pumping coins into the sturdy, wall-mounted phones. In the halls, students and staff walked head up, eyes were not peering down towards a cell phone. Some kids were listening to Walkman cassette players, swapping out tapes pulled from their pockets. The technology would be gone soon, becoming part of a museum display. Look at how people used to live, pay phones and cassette players.

He caught up with Stacy Randall who let him know she was scheduled to work at The Gap at the mall, a choice retail job. She apologized for not being able to make it to the game, but if she was a no-show at work, she was out of a job. He understood. She wasn't a big football fan anyway. They were a mismatched couple from the get-go. Things looked dim on that front. No matter, Jane should be there tonight. He would be looking for her, scanning the crowd during warmups. There was something special about that girl. She seemed like an old soul. Ken was surprised no one else had tried to connect with her. Maybe some guy did, and she brushed him off. Just as his grandparents had said. You have to make your move when something looks promising; advice taken.

Classes done for the day, he headed for the parking lot. The scene was like the morning but louder. This was Friday afternoon. Kids were hitting the ground running. Music was blaring, and the hair seemed even longer than just hours before. Heck, maybe it grew during the day. He smiled at that thought. Enjoy that hair, fellas. For many of you it will become sparse in short time. Use the Goody comb while you can.

He covered the walk home quickly, taking in the beauty of the fall. The weather was perfect for the game. This was a fantasy coming true. When mulling over the theories debated on *Across the Globe*, Ken had concluded it was all pipe dreams. Yet here he was walking down the street headed to the old household on game day. The long-established routine in full effect. He would get something to eat, say goodbye to his mother, and head back for warmups. There was something he was really looking forward to besides blasting down the field: the speech. George King's pregame talks were always awesome. Time stood still for a few moments as one voice filled the room. Much more than pregame hype, King would dig into the psyche of his players. The man was a bit of a Zen master, no doubt about that. He had the ability to make his players believe in themselves and want to win for him and his coaches. Ken would enjoy the speech as much as the actual playing time, the memories intertwined.

At home, he headed to the kitchen, his usual first stop. There was a note on the counter from his mother. She and his father would not be home before he headed out and would see him at the game. Handwritten notes were the way to communicate in those days. It would be close to a decade before email became omnipresent. Cell phones were years away. Business types and a few well-off kids might have mobile phones which were then called "car phones." They were bulky, way too big to carry around, so they stayed in the car. Plus, reception was spotty and billed by the minute. The cost of use was high. There was leftover chicken casserole to be heated up in the microwave. That technology was available by then, although the early units looked more like old-school TV sets. He would enjoy a quiet snack for a quick fuel-up before the big game.

Ken realized one issue was about to come to the forefront: the play calling. Granted, the offense the team ran was not complicated, and he wasn't the quarterback or pass receiver, who were part of the more intricate plays. However, it was sure to show up as soon as they began warmups. He grabbed the old bookbag and there it was, the playbook. As he ate the reheated casserole, he perused the book, and it started coming back. The team ran a lot of sweeps to the right and left and rushed the ball up the middle, off the tackle. The team relied on Ken's speed more than brute force to move the ball. He should be able to pull it off. He had to remember just a few of the go-to plays and ask questions about the others. The quarterback would know. Steve Hayes always had an answer. Steve was a decent kid. He was another classmate Ken had not seen or heard about in years, but he was surely doing well. The guy had a knack for landing on his feet. They would be catching up shortly, that was for sure.

As Ken approached the campus, jitters rushed through his body, and his heart was beating faster. It was all good. This was a fun time. Everything was going to be all right. Positive thinking had pushed him through games going back to the Pop Warner days. Negative thoughts bring bad results. Think about winning and it will happen, in most cases anyway. That was Ken's experience, and he wasn't changing his mindset now, not tonight. He recalled that Colonial won this one, not easily, but a win is what counts. Could that change? He didn't see how unless he did something stupid and screwed it up. His thoughts turned to the late-night radio chatter regarding going back in time. Was it possible for him to change what had already happened? He definitely did not dwell on that, not now. It could throw him off his game. Time to sit back and enjoy it. He was getting what he had wished for.

When he walked into the locker room it all came back, especially the dank smell. The fall air may have been the ultimate refresher. This was quite the opposite. The cleaning crew tried to counter it with bleach, but that created a mingled stink of body odor and chlorine. Oh, how the memories came back with sensory overload.

"Hey, Kenny, haven't seen much of you today."

Steve Hayes was rallying the troops. He had a calming effect on the team, which was a big reason King had slotted him into the QB spot. Steve did not have a big arm, but they didn't need that. They had Ken.

"Here and ready to go, buddy. Same smell this place always has, isn't it, Steve?"

"Sure, Ken, why would it smell any different?

You think Coach King plans on putting air freshener in our lockers?"

Ken realized he'd slipped up. He was letting on that he hadn't been around the foul aroma in a long time. He should have been used to this, a daily experience for the players. He caught himself and corrected the error.

"No, I guess it just really stands out tonight since the air is so crisp outside. Good weather for the lungs to operate in."

"Oh yeah, Ken, perfect night."

As the quarterback and his running back put their gear on, others in the room were already amping up, hooting and hollering, banging off lockers. Ken and Steve were the calm type, saving their energy for the field, for the actual game. Ken found it funny that some of the loudest teammates were often mediocre players. Perhaps they were compensating for their lack of impact on the game. It was harmless enough, and if it made them feel better, so be it. The same could be said for many in the stands. All too often the loudest, most obnoxious fans had no time on the field in any sport. Ken Sr. liked to remind his son how "the guys with the biggest mouths are often nowhere near the field. They play from the safety of the stands." It was a fair point, but Ken appreciated the fact the kids and parents came out. So what if they were a bit rambunctious at times, at least they showed up and supported the team.

It was dusk as the team hit the field for stretching. The lights were already on, and spectators were filing in. The bigger games drew early crowds. Ken's mom was in the concession stand setting up. This would be a money maker for the booster club. The parents had been at it since the kids were in elementary school, keeping the programs going so the kids had something to do. It had become a part of the families' social lives, with good friendships established. For most parents and players, it would all be over soon. Seniors were down to their last games. Even Ken, one of the best players in the council, would see it all end in a few weeks. A couple of colleges had reached out to him, but he got no serious scholarship offers. His grades didn't open any doors, and his play, while very good for high school, was not at the Division 1 level. What mattered now was to keep winning, to stay alive in the sectional playoffs with the ultimate goal being the state championship game. Colonial hadn't made it that far in many years. It was a long shot, but either way, the further they went, the more games the seniors would get before calling it a wrap for good. They all wanted to keep this train going.

While running through plays after stretching out, Ken had some rough spots, just as he envisioned. The quarterback noted this and was a bit concerned.

"What's up, Ken? You nervous?" Ken was always in sync with the plays. Something was off tonight.

"I'll be OK. I'm just a little sentimental. Steve, just think this will all be over soon. We have been at this since grammar school."

"I've been thinking about it all year."

"I think the key is to just enjoy it, take it all in."

"We got this, Kenny. We are going out winners."

Things smoothed out with generous amounts of verbal encouragement from Coach King and his staff. They were screaming. Ken thought they would lose their voices before the game started. King pulled him aside.

"You all right? I knew I saw something different in you with that speech today. You gone soft on me?" King was only half kidding. This wasn't the Kenny Heet he knew. Something was a bit off.

"I got it, Coach. I am going to turn it on tonight."

"Good. Do me a favor and start now. You are making me nervous."

Things smoothed out with Ken regaining his form. The plays were not too complex. After a few run-throughs he was up to speed. He was making his blocks and cutting his routes.

By the conclusion of warmups and play-runs, fans had filled in on both sides of the field. Both the home and visiting teams had big turnouts tonight. Ken peeked over at the student section, which was packed. Jane was sitting towards the bottom of the bleachers. It looked like she had come alone. She had such a mature demeanor, almost like a parent sitting with the kids. Ken wondered if she was doing some time traveling herself, an adult visiting the kid zone. Well, wouldn't that make a great story for David Sphere's radio show. Two time travelers unknowingly running into each other. No time to worry about that now. He gave her a quick wave, and she waved back. It was time to head to the locker room for Coach King's pregame speech.

* * *

The room was quiet. The players crammed into three-quarters of a circle, some standing, some kneeling. The coaches filled out the front of the circle with King front and center. Other memories of the time were foggy, but not this; this was an often-repeated scene in Ken's mind. He was once again in the middle of it. He was glad he came back.

"You don't wish for things to happen. You make them happen. Nobody said life was fair or easy, and if they did, they lied to you. That is why we practice as much and as hard as we do. It is why so many of you put in all the work on your own time, off-season and on. That is what separates us from other teams, the work we put into it. Well, the team we're up against does the same. I'm not going to stand up here and tell you we are going to walk all over them. I would be blowing smoke up your butts. If I tell you this is a cakewalk, then some of you would be doubting yourself when they start pushing back. And they will push back. But we will push harder, running the plays the way we practiced, with everyone doing their part. We prepared for this game. No corners were cut. Now it is up to each of you, picking one another up, moving together as a team. Play after play, drive after drive, series after series, we keep it up and grind them down. Simple as that. We do that and we win."

A few seconds of silence. Then King continued.

"We are proud of every one of you in this room. Conduct yourselves like men, and you will have our respect, win or lose. You have all given your time and effort while others stood off to the side. You stepped up. You have been at this for a long time. For many of you, the playing time is winding down. We want to keep rolling, keep it going to get as much game time as possible out of this season. All of you know our ultimate goal. Keep your heads up before, during, and after the game. Now let's go."

The room erupted. King's words were said with certainty and clarity. He was honest, not vulgar, and sincere beyond a doubt. That is what Ken loved about the man. He had respect for anyone, on any team, who put forth the effort to compete in a tough game. He carried himself with dignity on and off the field, and it rubbed off on his players. Most certainly on Ken Heet.

* * *

There were players who could recall the action, in detail, in games that took place years ago. That wasn't Ken's thing. He remembered the big losses and the big plays and of course the wins, but if quizzed on the details, he often came up empty. He had tried to move on with life, but he did love the opportunity in front of him at this moment. He knew they won this big game against Little Falls. Could things change tonight? Was it possible for Colonial to lose, if they had already won? The scenarios discussed on David Sphere's program came to mind. Ken would find out soon enough.

The team lined up for entry to the field. Ken was up front with Steve. The two seniors would lead the team out. The players jogged from the main campus across a grass field to the field's entry gate. When they hit the gate, they ran. Queen's "We Will Rock You" blared over the PA system. An air horn shrieked. The crowd roared. It was just as he remembered, and it was a blast. After the game, after the spectators filed out and the players were gone, there would be silence. Same thick turf, same bright lights, but empty bleachers. It was the people that made the moments great, not the manicured field.

After circling the field letting out giant screams of excitement, they headed for the sidelines. A female student belted out the national anthem. Ken took one more look into the stands and again spotted Jane. She did not look super enthused, but at least she showed up. He hoped to put on a good show for a girl at her first football game.

Ken and Steve walked out to the middle of the field for the coin toss. They called heads, and heads it was. Next thing you know, Ken was in the backfield waiting to receive the kickoff. Little Falls, well aware of his speed, booted the ball away from him. It bounced out of the hands of his teammate on the other side and landed out of bounds. Not an auspicious start, but at least Colonial retained possession.

On the first play from scrimmage, the defense was staring Ken down, all expecting he would get the ball. But Coach King called an unusual play. A short pass attempt to the end, which was completed, for a two-yard gain. Ken could not recall the player's name but was sure he was an underclassman. At least the kid didn't drop it. Now all eyes were really on Ken. No way Colonial puts the ball up in the air again. Sure enough, an off-tackle play was called and Ken picked up an easy five yards. Right back in the swing of things. Three more needed for a first down. Ken got it again, this time a sweep to the left, and away he went. First down and more. Oh, the joy, the sounds, the smell, the cool night air. The Heet was back. However, there was something else Ken could feel. These guys could tackle. No arm tackles or shirt grabs, these guys were squaring up, lowering the hips, and bringing it on, especially a nasty linebacker, 58, who was hitting hard.

On it went, back and forth. High school football, especially during Ken's playing days, was most often straightforward, with the offense run-based, an occasional swing pass and some long passes, rarely completed. On this night the teams would grind it out. Ken would play some defense, going in as a defensive back and returning the favor with his own hits, but he was predominantly a ball mover.

Football is a team sport at heart. On the third possession Ken managed to put the ball in the end zone with the help of a solid block on 58, the Eagles hard- hitting linebacker. Who was that kid?

The boys from Little Falls responded with their own running touchdown, and it was back and forth. The scoreboard kept the tally and time. On most possessions both teams came up empty, putting no points on the board. Neither side had an accurate kicker. To score via field goal they had to get close to the end zone. Neither team did. This was not the typical game with Ken running wild, chewing up yards. He was up against a stout, well-couched defense. They weren't giving up anything without a fight. He was feeling it in his legs and midsection, where the hits landed hard. This was a tough way to relive a memory. He had landed in a brutal game for his trek back in time.

At halftime, the score was tied at 13-13, unlucky numbers. Colonial and Little Falls each had two touchdowns but missed one of the extra points. Ken scored both of Colonial's touchdowns. Those were the toughest points he had ever come by.

Back in the locker room, Coach King's half-time motivational ramp-up was short.

"I told you guys this wasn't going to be easy. We can do this. If we keep at them, they will wear down. Our cardio will win it. I like what I am seeing from an aggression standpoint. We have to get the blocks where they need to be."

When saying that, King shot a quick gaze towards Ken. Perhaps he was attempting to let his running back know, more help is on the way. He needed him to make the plays and move the ball into the end zone.

Ken was thinking more about 58 than any pep talk. He had to stay away from that kid. When the group talk was over, King pulled Ken aside.

"How are you feeling, Kenny? You took a couple of shots out there. You usually avoid those."

"Yeah, it's 58. He is the one. Get guys on him and I can score more."

"We will take care of it. Ken, I am proud of you. You are playing hard. This game gets a little dangerous sometimes." King said that with a cat's smile, aiming to soften the blows.

"It isn't so dangerous. Coach, the most dangerous thing any of us do is drive around in a car. That is what can hurt you bad. You have to be careful with that."

It had just come out. That was as much warning as Ken could give Coach King. He could not say, "I came back in time. You are going to get killed by a drunk driver…" King would have pulled him from the game thinking his running back had suffered a concussion. He had no response to Ken's comment. He slapped him on the pads and moved on to talk with his coaches.

Ken didn't recall the game being this tough. Perhaps 58 traveled back in time too and decided things were going to be different this time, changing the outcome with his efforts alone. It didn't matter now. Ken would do whatever it took to win. He didn't come back to lose what had already been won.

The team charged back onto the field with a little less wind behind their sails but determined. Often that is all it takes, determination. Ken looked to the stands and there sat Jane. He was happy to see she stayed for the second half. She was getting to see a heck of a game her first time out. Ken noted King was with the offensive line coach, taking some extra time to talk with the boys from the O line and another running back, Jack Young, a junior, who Ken didn't know well. The underclassman came late to the game of football, not having played through the youth leagues. He was very fast, a natural athlete. Ken assumed King was telling them they must block better, and key on 58, the one-man wrecking crew. Ken hoped they listened. If they didn't, he might not make it to the end of the game. Imagine finishing out his dream game laid out on the sidelines. He could not think like that, a losing attitude could be self-fulfilling.

The whistle blew. The boys from Little Falls must have gotten quite a halftime speech because they came out on fire. They scored on their first possession and made the point after. It was now 20-13. Their drive was unnerving. Ken and the boys had to keep pace, or things could go downhill quickly.

Coach King was fired up. He was letting loose. He rarely got this loud on the sidelines. Ken was sure Jane heard the ranting and was thinking "What happened to that nice health class teacher? Some demon has entered his soul."

King's roar had its intended effect. On the next kickoff, Jack Young caught the ball and darted up the field. He wasn't looking for blockers. The junior running back took off on his own as if a jetpack was propelling him. Ken loved it, someone else was getting some ball time, a rest for his bones at least for one play. Young took a smart route and stayed clear of 58 who was on the other side of the field, broke two tackles, and scored. Even Jane popped up out of her seat on that play.

Holy crap! Ken thought it was awesome and smart. When a player is that good, stay the hell away from him. If machismo comes into play with the "You ain't so bad attitude" taking over, things can go downhill, painfully so. The underclassman made the right moves and put points on the board. Colonial's kicker delivered the extra point. All even at 20-20. They had a hell of a game going with lots of time to go.

King cooled. The screaming was gone for the moment. Colonial was staying with Little Falls. That was Step 1. Step 2 was to hold them down. Step 3 was to score again, ideally close to the end of regulation time.

The next sequence of downs, on both sides, produced a stalemate. The clock was running. The fourth quarter was underway. Both teams were tired. Colonial's vaunted cardio, a characteristic of King's teams, was being pushed to the limit. There were no easy series of downs. Every snap was contested. Seeing his grandparents was awesome and he would take their advice with him, but the game had become more a grind than a walk down memory lane.

The teams were creeping into the final minutes of the game, still tied. Ken didn't want to go into overtime. Nobody did. Not Even 58, the terror of the field, could be looking forward to that. Set aside the fatigue, to lose in overtime would be crushing.

With the final two minutes on the clock, Little Falls took a risk to try to catch the defense off guard. They put the ball in the air, going deep. The Falls quarterback torqued his arm back and let loose. The wide receiver downfield reached out for a one-hand grab. There was a gasp from the home crowd as he continued to move with the ball in his left hand clenched to his chest. But as he brought up his right hand to secure possession, the ball popped out. There may have been some dew on the football since it was getting cooler as the night went on. Perhaps it was simply nerves. Either way the receiver coughed the ball up. It was a fumble.

Ken could sense the horror flowing through the mind of that kid in the split second when the ball, after a great catch, flew out of his hands and to the ground at the fifty-yard line. Jack Young, who was now playing defensive back, pounced on the loose ball. The shocked wide receiver immediately fell on top of him. But Jack had possession. Colonial's ball, less than two minutes to go, fifty yards from the end zone. They wanted to put the ball in the end zone, the surest way to win. A missed field goal would most likely send the teams into overtime. Put it in the end zone and go home winners.

Ken and the boys were back on the field and the crowd was going wild. He had never heard it this loud. Jane Warner was getting a treat. The first play was a quick seven-yard pick-up when Ken swept around the right side with you know who slamming into him with all he had left. It was the hardest hit Ken took thus far. The next play Coach King threw Jack Young a bone. His name was called for a run up the middle off tackle. He got the first down by inches. The clock was at 1:08. Forty yards to go and it was their game. One more time to Ken, who took it up the middle again for another five. Then Steve made a T with his hands for a timeout. Just under a minute now. King called the QB to the sideline for a quick huddle.

"I don't want to wait too long. They probably think we are going to run another short gain play for another first up the middle. We will sell them the middle run but sweep it left and have Ken put it in. Switchback left is the play. We will have time for another shot or two if we are short. But if we get in now, we can hold them off for the win."

"Got it, Coach. We will try to fake out 58."

"Exactly. Pull 58 in. Line up like Ken is coming up the middle and cut around, switchback left. Steve, call it, and make sure the line knows, sell the middle run." King wasn't one for trick plays, this being an adventurous call for the conservative minded coach. The team had run it at practice, but rarely used the play in a game. King was relying on the element of surprise and the speed of Ken to make it work.

Steve trotted out to the huddle passing along the directives of King.

"All right, we are going for it now. Switchback left. Jack, blast through like you are making a hole, the line moves with you. Ken, fake the follow and sweep left and take it in. Coach wants to go in on this play."

Steve would not usually detail the play in the huddle. His players should know them by heart. In this case he wanted to be sure all were on the same page.

Ken knew If he could cut the corner and get away from 58 he was going to cross the goal line. He wasn't relying on a block. He had to make 58 think he was coming up the middle and then slip around the side. But he had been sweeping left all night. Switching to the right could be the little extra something that made it work. If it didn't and the coach complained, Ken would tell him he saw a lane right and took it. He had never done it before, never diverged from a play from any coach, let alone George King. If he got in, all would be forgiven. There would not be much initial blocking for him anyway, regardless of which way he ran. The line was selling the middle run. He was getting in the end zone on this play. He would make it happen.

Ken's heart was racing. He recalled winning this game, but something else was going on tonight, much more dramatic than anything in his recollection. Ken lined up in the backfield, same as last time, set for a run up the middle. He looked right into the eyes of 58 as if to say, "I am coming right at you." The look was returned; 58 wanted Ken to come right at him.

Set, hut, hut, hike! Steve slammed the ball into Ken's hands as Jack Young blasted forward as if he was making a hole for Ken to snake through. Ken moved behind him. The offensive line surged forward, and 58 sprung to fill the hole he was sure Ken was coming through. Ken cut to the right, giving it everything he had in an all-out effort to get around the edge and down the field. He gave a quick glance to his left and saw 58 moving forward. It was working! He had an open field to barrel towards the end zone. Another quick look over his shoulder to make sure 58 hadn't caught on. The big hitter hadn't, but the peek was a mistake. Ken faked out 58, but the linebacker's teammate 45 was not fooled. The defensive back had picked up Ken's cut and was shooting at him at an angle, coming in like a missile.

Ken never saw it. He had locked in on one player forgetting there were ten more defenders on the field. Ken, King, and the entire offense had concentrated on one player and it cost them. Ken got nailed hard, knocked clear out of bounds, but he held on to the ball. The whistle blew. Ken Heet was down on the sideline, not moving. He was out cold. The cheering stopped.

9

BACK IN TIME

Ken's eyes opened to a blur. He could see light, but nothing was in focus. Where the hell was he? Now he really began to think he had died. He started to breathe heavily, practically hyperventilating. Then he heard a voice.

"Ken, Ken, thank God, you're back!"

He recognized the voice as his vision began to clear. Bill Powers was standing over him.

"Nurse, nurse, he is awake!"

What the hell happened? The last he knew he was playing in a football game.

"Oh, thank God, Ken! My prayers were answered. I have to start going to church again."

"What happened?" Ken's voice was weak, barely audible.

"You got hit with a big chunk of ice. You were knocked out, unconscious. We were moving the trailers. Some ice shot off the top of one and hit you square in the head. Ken, I thought we lost you."

A nurse entered the room, stepped in front of

Bill Powers, and looked directly into Ken's eyes.

"Mr. Heet, you are at Columbia Medical Center. You have been out for a while." She held his hands and applied light pressure. "Can you squeeze my hands?" Ken did so. She pushed on the bottom of his right and left feet. "Can you push back on my hands with your feet?" He did that too, no problem.

"Very good, Mr. Heet. We thought you were OK from a cervical standpoint, no spinal issues. You have control of movement, excellent. Can you see me clearly?"

"At first, no I couldn't, but things are clearing up."

"That's to be expected. You were out for a bit. Your boss has been here the whole time."

Bill Powers looked haggard. A grey stubble had formed over his cheeks and chin. His hair was matted.

"How long have you been here, Bill?"

"Since it happened. I came in right behind the ambulance. I spent Christmas here, so a couple of days."

"Oh man, go home to your wife. Can someone get this collar off my neck?"

"Soon enough Mr. Heet. Let's get the doctor in here first. We have a neurologist on the floor."

"OK, but, Bill, please go home now. I will be OK."

"You don't feel anything? Nothing hurts?" Bill Powers had assumed his friend would wake up in pain.

"My head hurts, sure, but as you saw, I can move everything. Hands, fingers, feet. I will be OK. I have a tough noggin, buddy. Get some rest, Bill. I am sure your family misses you."

Bill looked relieved, like the weight of the world had been lifted off his shoulders. He stepped back and sat down for a minute to gather his thoughts.

"All right, Kenny, but I'll be back after I clean up and get some rest."

* * *

"Hello Mr. Heet, I'm Dr. Howard Davis. I am the resident neurologist. You, sir, are a lucky man. You are bouncing back extremely well. When people come out of a coma, even short ones like you had, they are usually not coherent. It generally takes time, and some people…"

Dr. Davis could have stepped out of central casting. He was a mature, distinguished-looking man with a full head of salt-and-pepper, closed-cropped hair. He wore a crisp white lab coat. His glasses were stylish, and his highly shined shoes were sticking out of the cuffed bottoms of tailored slacks. The man had presence.

"Well, doctor, I have a hard head. I have taken some hard hits in my life and have handled them well. Are you implying some people are never the same after a coma?"

"There are often effects that linger, sometimes permanently. Do you recall what happened to you?"

"At first no, no I didn't. But after my boss explained it, I now remember what happened. It was an accident. Things like that happen. I just feel bad for my boss. I am happy Bill went home. The guy looked horrible."

"That's nice, Mr. Heet. You are a considerate man, thinking of others when you are banged up. How do you feel physically? Any severe pains? Your neurological movements seem fine. That is extremely encouraging."

"My head hurts, that's for sure, but I've felt worse. I would like to get this collar off my neck."

"We can do that soon. Let's see if we can get you up, feet on the ground, and a walk with assistance. If you can do that, we can really get things moving."

"Sounds great, doctor. I do have a question."

"Sure, what is it?"

"Is it common for people who were out like I was, for as long as I was, to have dreams? I mean vivid dreams."

"Well, Mr. Heet, research and textbooks will say no. The brain shuts down and that is that. You breathe and circulate blood, but for the rest of the activity in your brain, the switch is off, lights are out."

Ken returned a perplexed look but said nothing.

"That being said, I have been doing this for a long time, and let me tell you, textbooks and studies, they don't know everything. Mr. Heet, I have had many patients tell me they had very vivid, very memorable dreams. So, I guess the answer is, it seems to be possible in one form or the other. I am assuming you had such dreams."

"Oh yeah, yes I did."

Ken left it at that. No sense going back and forth with Dr. Davis. It was best to get his recovery going and get the hell out of this hospital. He had no desire to be here, never liked the antiseptic smell of the place.

"Doctor, whatever you need me to do to get moving and get out of here as soon as possible, I will do it. No disrespect to the hospital, but it isn't for me."

"Understood, Mr. Heet. Hospitals aren't hotels. We are happy to take care of you, but we too would like to see you go home, when that's safe of course. But we can't take this lightly. Give us some time for a proper evaluation, and if all looks good, we will get you home."

"Good deal. Let's get to work then."

* * *

As promised, Bill Powers returned after a nap, a shower, and a change of clothes.

"Ken, I feel responsible for this. That is why I stayed here. I called your folks, tracked them down from your employee records. Your dad has not been feeling well, but they are both coming back. I told them to give it a day. No sense having your dad, who is sick himself, come to a hospital. Please give them a call."

"Got it, Bill. I will do that right away. What's the problem with my dad?"

"He is having issues with his back, lots of pain, according to your mother. It is difficult for him to travel."

Ken figured the years of sports had finally caught up with his dad. Additionally, the man had a fairly physical job, especially when he was younger. He worked his way up to construction foreman but paid his dues to get there. Ken wondered if years down the road, he too would deal with physical ailments from the days of his youth. The ice chunk to the head could also come back to nag him some day.

"Bill, this was an accident. Stuff happens all the time. We are outside, in the elements, it is bound to happen."

"Right Ken, but I am your boss. I have been there a long time. It is my job to be aware of stuff like this and keep my people out of harm's way."

"Ain't gonna happen, Bill, no way. Things happen, regardless of how safe we try to be."

"What did the doctor say? What is the prognosis?"

"He said I was lucky I had a hard head and was 'rugged.' Yes, that was the phrase he used. Sounds like a term for a guy in an antiperspirant commercial. He seems to think I will be good. I need to walk around, give them a little dog-and-pony show, not pee my pants, and I should be good to go in another day or two. They are going to run some more tests, I'm sure of that."

"And that's that?"

"Yep, that's it. As soon as they clear me, I can come back to work. Think of all the overtime I am missing."

"It will be there when you get back, no rush. You think about going down to see your folks?"

"Sure, now that you tell me my dad's back hurts, I should go down. I will have to get down before it gets too hot at their place. I can't stand the heat, Bill."

"Sounds like a plan. Now I do have to get going. You know it is still busy, and of course we are down one of our best men."

"One of the best?"

"OK, our best man."

"That's more like it, Bill. I will be back soon." They both smiled. Ken was banged up, but he still had his sense of humor.

* * *

Just as Dr. Davis promised, Ken was put through the paces. It all went well. He was given a clean bill of health. Ken wasn't cleared for work yet, but he got the go-ahead to rest at home.

"Well, Mr. Heet, things look good. CAT scan looks fine, a contusion to your head of course, but you took it well. Seems like you have a high threshold for pain. Most would be demanding pain medication at this point."

"I've always been like that doctor. Ibuprofen usually does the trick for me. I have never needed much more than that."

"Good, very good. Painkillers cause problems for some people."

"Oh yeah, I listen to the news. I've heard the stories."

"Well, tomorrow you go home, Mr. Heet. We will have to set you up with a ride. No driving yet."

"Sure, absolutely, no problem. Please do me a favor. Arrange for a cab for the ride home. I don't want to bother my boss anymore."

"OK, the staff can take care of that."

"Doctor, thanks for the good care. You know the saying: 'If we have our health…'"

"We have everything. Yes, a true statement. We will schedule a return visit at my office in the medical building next door. We want to make sure there are no changes, no issues."

"Then I can be cleared for work?"

"Yes, after a return visit. Your employer may have a different policy. You are a driver, correct?"

"Yes, but not over the road, not even on the road for the most part. I work on site."

"Well, they may have their own medical people who want to see you."

"We will figure it out."

Ken knew damn well his employer would be happy to see him back in the saddle as soon as possible. If he didn't come back with a workers compensation claim, they would be ecstatic. He had no plans to do that, wasn't his style. He fell back into the hospital bed. Ken may have been in Neverland for a couple of days, but he still needed some rest. They'd had him up and down the hallways and staircases, checking his balance and breathing. It wasn't much, not like the runs and wind sprints of his youth, but it was enough now to make him want to slumber a bit more.

He dozed off, but this time there were no dreams, at least nothing he would remember. It was a peaceful rest.

* * *

When he arrived home his dog was not there. His co-workers had looked out for him. One of the guys operated a kennel on the side and he gladly volunteered to take care of Skipper, the loyal mixed breed, until Ken was back up and running. Bill Powers had delegated the job to the kennel operator. That was a huge favor. Ken owed the men.

He had the cab driver stop at a sub shop on the way home. He wanted some nonhospital food and was sure nothing in his refrigerator was edible. Upon returning home he entered a lonely household. Skipper was not at the door to greet him. Ken would get his dog back soon, a high priority.

As he sat in his well-worn recliner, eating a chicken sandwich, Ken ran through what transpired over the last handful of days. It was extra quiet now, decompression time. Was this series of events worthy of his first call to David Sphere? "Hello David, I didn't travel through time, but man did I come close." No, he would keep this to himself. Perhaps he'd lay a little of it on Bill Powers, letting his supervisor know the ice chunk to the head wasn't all bad. He got to spend some quality time with grandparents, even If it was in La La Land. He'd tell Bill not to feel bad. Some good advice was picked up from the unfortunate experience.

What exactly was accurate about the dreamscape? The football side of it was spot on for the most part, including the ending. It wasn't something Ken liked to think about, but his football-playing time did indeed end on the sidelines. That was reality. Often when looking back at the days of yore, it is done through rose-colored glasses with the downside of events repressed. Ken had spent what was left of the game sitting on a bench with butterflies fluttering around his head; 45 did what 58 could not. He knocked Ken out of that game, and out of the next two, the final games of the season for Colonial High School. Ken missed the opportunity to play in the section championship game the following week, a victory, and the game after that, a tough loss in the opening round of the state championship bracket.

Coach King would not put him back in, not after a concussion. Even if it wasn't state protocol at the time, King would never take that risk. Ken was fortunate he wasn't hurt permanently after that wallop.

Jack Young had stepped up on the next play and put the ball in the end zone for the victory over Little Falls. Numbers 58 and 45 walked over to check on Ken after it was over, offering a handshake. He knew damn well who 58 was. Sam Freeman was well known as one of the hardest hitters in the council. Ken, Coach King, and the entire team knew who 58 was and the problems he caused opponents. In the dream he was a nameless boogie man, chasing Ken all over the field. Perhaps that was Ken's mind telling him to forget about Freeman, put it all out of his memory. The linebacker was just a number. The mysteries of the human mind. Riddles that will never be solved. Sam Freeman ended up in a similar situation to Ken. A very good player, but one who didn't move on to collegiate play. He had no idea what happened to Sam after high school. Likely he was employed at a job very similar to Ken's depot post.

Jack Young went on to play well the next two weeks and his final year of high school ball filling Ken's shoes. Ken recalled Jack would play four years of D3 ball at an out-of-state college. He wasn't sure what happened to him after that, but he likely did well for himself. Jack was a go-getter for sure and likely fared well at his chosen profession.

Ken had not in fact strayed from the play called by Coach King. He ran to the left as instructed. Perhaps his mind, in that dream, had pushed for a different route in hopes of a different ending. But there was no different ending. He still took a hard hit forcing him out of the game. Now while convalescing from the accident at the depot, Ken did something he had never done before; he researched the results of that final season. Digging into records that were easier to access nowadays, a trip to the library no longer needed, he found some local news links confirming the reality of his final playing days. He knew what he was going to find to bring some more closure to events he didn't care to think about. Sure, he had relished the idea of going back in time and reliving all the great games, but with that came the bad plays, and the final one. It was time to put that all to bed.

Additionally, there was the sad reality of what happened to Coach King. Fortunately, the dream never got that far, not to that ghastly event. Ken had no desire to go through that memorial ceremony again, even if only in his mind. It was a terribly sad ending for a man who had so much more to give to the community. Many lesser souls walk around while George King died on the side of the road before reaching the age of fifty.

There were events in that dream that certainly did not happen, at least not in Ken's memory. He never had such a conversation with his grandparents. He did recall seeing them walk hand in hand on daily excursions in the neighborhood, but never had a heart-to-heart talk with them, at least not like the dream. He assumed that was his mind, sculpting what his brain thought they would say if he ever had asked them the questions. What a waste of a great source of information, all the knowledge the elders have. His mind was reaching into that mentally created advice session to correct an omission.

Also, the speech to the class did indeed happen. He did recall giving a presentation in health class, probably revolving around perfusion, but it was nothing dramatic. It was a topic that Ken found fascinating. There had been no pleas to enjoy the little things or any reference to his grandparents. He did remember Coach King giving him a pat on the back, an attaboy for the presentation. As in the dream, Ken never made the honor roll when report cards were handed out, so that might explain King taking the time to give the mediocre student some praise. The gesture had stood out in Ken's thoughts over the years.

Lastly, the important part and what Ken found the most significant aspect of the entire episode. Jane Warner was real, and he was sure she was in that health class. She was a bright student, and Ken would not have been in other classes with her. But as a quiet girl, she was barely noticed in that class and the school in general. She had a pleasant way about her, never bothered anyone, went about her business in a studious manner and was, as he recalled, very pretty. She never made any attempt to bring attention to herself. "Plain Jane" would be a fair play on her name back in those days. Ken noticed, but never said a word to her. Jane was a calm, classy girl, likely now the same as a woman. He was, as in the dream, dating Stacy back then, so he would have been less likely to chat up Jane Warner. He certainly didn't invite her to the football game. There was an intimidation factor with her being so smart. He wouldn't have wanted to embarrass himself with an awkward conversation. "Hey, hello smart girl with a promising future. Want to come see me run around a football field? I might even get knocked senseless!" He didn't imagine that conversation going anywhere. What does one talk about with the brainiest students? Ken didn't know. He's never tried.

Here he was, back in the present, with things as they were, albeit with a banged-up noggin. First off, he had to get Skipper back. God, he missed that dog. He was sure Skip missed him too. They'd been best friends since he picked up the puppy at an adoption fair at the local shelter. The best place to get a dog. Ken was convinced of that.

Time to get on with life. He would take the advice given by his grandparents in the other-world conversation they had. He wasn't old. There were a lot of years to come. He had his health. The whole experience had been a wake-up call to that fact. The hit he took to the head from the ice could have caused permanent damage. He would try for some more Ken time, take the advice he had given out in an imaginary presentation in a time long past. He now had his feet planted in reality. The longing to get in one more game ended up being a small part of his trip back. The playing time was trivial. What was important was the time spent with family members now gone and a chance to talk with a girl he failed to notice when walking the halls of the old school. Those were the highlights of the trip for sure.

IN THE SWING OF THINGS

Skipper was happy to see his owner, and Ken even happier to claim his best friend. He didn't have to make a trip to the kennel. His co-worker dropped Skipper off at Ken's place. The kennel crew was thoughtful. They groomed Ken's best friend, and clipped his nails. The mutt looked sharp. He and his K9 companion got right back into a routine. It was actually better than before. With the required time off from work, they were able to take two, three, or more walks throughout the day. They developed a comfortable stride. The days of Skipper tugging on the leash were gone. They walked in tandem now. Ken's grandfather may have had his beloved wife to walk with, but Ken had Skipper, a nice runner-up in the competition for life companions.

The days passed by quickly. Ken's follow-up with Dr. Howard Davis went well, no issues at all.

"Well, Mr. Heet, things look fine. Those daily walks you are taking with your dog have helped greatly. I tell all my patients, really anyone who will listen, walking is the best exercise. It is also the safest."

Ken had said the same when presenting his thoughts to his classmates during his dream. The doctor was preaching to the choir.

"Absolutely, doctor, I have been saying that for years."

"Usually, at this point, I would recommend light duty work only, but…"

"But you think I am ready to go? Also, please call me Ken, doctor. We are getting used to each other, but I will still call you doctor." Ken laughed, though he would indeed still refer to Davis as "doctor." Being a man of little academic success, Ken revered those accomplished in the fields of medicine.

"I will sign off on it, but please, Ken, take it slow. I believe you will need a full physical for your commercial driver's license. I assume your employer will set that up or require you to do it."

"Yes, we are required to have those every two years, but I will likely need to have another before I am fully cleared."

"You say your driving is limited to a yard or parking lots? I mean for the big trucks, the rigs."

"Absolutely, that is my realm, doctor. The confines of a fenced-in depot lot. I spend most of my time in a small area. I do plan to get out more, get up in the mountains for some hikes, maybe some travel."

"Excellent, excellent, Ken. So many patients I have had over the years come to the same conclusion after an event like this. Many in much worse shape than you, their options for adventure limited, but they still want to get out and live more, take it all in."

"It is too bad things like a chunk of ice to the head have to bring people to such decisions."

"Hard learned lessons for sure."

* * *

The time off was welcomed, the daily walks with Skipper refreshing, but Ken knew he had to get back to work. He was cleared for duty after a full physical, his credentials as a Class A driver were up to snuff. It was time to give Bill Powers a call.

"Hello Bill, I am good to go. These straight-time paychecks are pitiful. I need to get back on the overtime train and make some real money."

"I am glad you called, Kenny. I have been thinking about that for the last couple of days. Unsurprisingly, Carl Dade is out again. The trick back flared up again. We were short and now we are shorter."

Dade was notorious for phantom injuries that put him out of work for months at a clip. In Ken's and Bill Power's opinion, the guy was lazy. He might as well go out permanently and be done with it. Bill figured his own back was much worse than Carl Dade's, but he showed up every day.

"Well, I have my paperwork, my medical clearance, and I am good to go."

"Awesome, how is everything else going? Any new developments in your life?"

"Other than long walks with my dog, no. I have been thinking about the night shift though. Being off it and living a regular day schedule lately has made me feel like a normal human being again. I don't feel like a vampire. The antisocial vibe drifted away."

"You thinking about putting in for the shift?"

"I would miss my favorite supervisor, but yeah the thought has entered my mind."

"Me too. I don't have too long to go, five years max, maybe less than that. I have been thinking a move would be good. Some of the management on days will annoy the crap out of me and it is more hectic, but you have to take the good with the bad."

"Great, we can make the move together. That is what I hoped for."

"Fair enough. However, we have an immediate issue."

"You need me to come in early, and tomorrow would be a great time."

"You are psychic, my friend."

"Don't need to be a visionary to figure that out. What time do you need me to come in?"

"How about six p.m. tomorrow? I'll go easy on

you for starters. I won't get a full double shift out of you right off the rip."

"Got it. See you tomorrow at six."

Back in the saddle, for good, bad, or indifferent. It was like Ken never left.

* * *

It was winter, so Ken's scenic hiking trips could wait. He was happy to be heading back in at an overtime rate, and he was helping his friend Bill Powers. Back in the saddle and making some extra cash, nothing wrong with that. He headed in a little early, giving himself time to stop by the Quick Mart and pick up some snacks for the long night ahead. It was a routine that had been broken up by the whack to his head and the temporary departure from the real world, but he knew he would slide back in like he had never left.

He rolled into the mini-mart parking lot, on a typical dreary late winter day. It was already dark. There was slush all over the pavement, leftovers from recent storms. A few cars were lined up at the pumps with no one looking enthused about the weather and money being spent to keep the cars moving. Most of these drivers were on their way home from work, topping off their tanks for the following day's activity. Ken headed into the store, straight to the beverage cooler to grab some iced tea, a go-to beverage. His next stop would be to the snack aisle for calories to keep him going into the early morning hours.

As he made his way to the back of the store, he noticed a woman reaching into the cooler for a container of milk. It couldn't be, no way. She had hardly changed since high school. Some people are that way, maintaining a similar physical appearance for most of their lives. Ken was one of them. He wore the same size clothing he had in high school, a bit snugger fit, but he could swing it. Jane Warner shared those characteristics. He recognized her immediately. The literal woman of his dreams was standing ten feet away holding a half-gallon of two-percent milk. This was bizarre. He wondered for a second if he was dreaming again. He knew he wasn't, and he didn't hesitate. He had to say something.

"Jane Warner?"

She turned and looked, and he could tell she did not recognize him. Of course, she hadn't been smacked in the head with a chunk of ice and experienced a coma-fueled dream.

"I am sorry, you probably don't remember me, but we went to high school together. We were in a class together with my favorite teacher Mr. King, or Coach as I would have called him. He taught health class."

He was embarrassed now, thinking she had no idea who he was. Some creep in a mini-mart trying to strike up a conversation. She had a couple of items in her hand and a purse. In an act of chivalry, he quickly grabbed a small tote basket from a rack and offered it to her.

"Your hands look full. Maybe you could use this?"

"Thank you, yes, I picked up more than I planned to." She put the items in the basket while looking at him, trying to jar her memory.

"Sure, I do remember you. You played football. Mr. King was such a nice man."

She remembered him. This wasn't totally embarrassing, at least not yet.

"Yeah, football, little basketball too. I'm sorry I didn't tell you my name, Ken Heet."

"Yes, Ken Heet, I remember now. You look just like you did in high school."

"Same for you, which is why I recognized you so quickly." That and the fact you were a central character in a dream I just had.

"I am going to make a prediction. You are now an engineer or scientist of some sort."

"Huh, how did you know that?"

"You were always super smart. I figured you did well for yourself."

"Well, yes, I work in a lab. I work on research projects, nothing too exciting."

She was being modest, an admirable trait. He wasn't about to say, "I drive a truck, did great for myself too." He would hold that back. Still, he earned decent pay, so it really wasn't an embarrassing admission. Ken took a quick look at her hands and saw no rings. It didn't surprise him. If she was indeed unattached, it would have suited her introverted personality. Now what to do? This was getting awkward quickly.

"How about you, Ken? What have you been up to?"

Honesty is the best policy, Ken. Don't BS her.

"I am a union driver, been so for years. Actually, I am heading into work now. They called me in for overtime. Nothing special, but it pays the bills, keeps a roof over my head, and it is secure."

"Good. Security is good. I don't know if you are like me, but I gave up excitement for security. My job is mundane."

"You're telling me. I could write a book on mundane existence."

Chit-chat in the mini-mart has its limits. They were nearing the "time to move on" moment.

"Well, Jane, it was nice to see you. I don't see many high school classmates anymore. Haven't for years."

"Me neither. I didn't see many when I was there!" She laughed, then deadpanned. "I was a bit quiet."

"Well, it paid off. You certainly made your way in the world. You were looking downfield." Sports comment, not the best choice of words, but she took it well and smiled.

With no line at the checkout counter, they quickly paid. Ken said goodbye with a polite nod, and she returned a smile. They walked out into the cold air. Jane headed towards her car, a Volvo. Now, isn't that typical for an analytical type. Ken hesitated for a second, but he could not let this go, no way. What type of coincidence was this, running into her after all that had happened? What were the chances? He remembered his grandfather's words of advice: "Don't be hesitant, make a move."

He walked over to the Volvo and let it fly.

"Jane, this may be awkward, but would you like to go out for dinner sometime? As I was saying, I never see anyone from high school anymore. I work with guys older than me, or younger, but no peers. It would be nice to talk with someone from my era, shoot the breeze. Hey, I'll even meet you in a public place, less you think I'm a creep who picks up ladies at mini-marts."

The last line got her. He was trying to be funny, and it worked. Levity to the rescue.

"That's a good one! I don't get around much either. But sure, I will have dinner with you."

"Great, and I'll have you know I'll spare no expense. The Olive Garden is certainly on the table. I will put this overtime money to good use." That line got another laugh. Ken's sense of humor had matured a little. The OG not being the best pick for a romantic first date.

"You're funny, and I don't care where we go. It will be nice to get out."

"Sounds good, and I love the fact you picked up my attempt at humor. Not all people do. I have to get going, Jane. Work awaits. I'll give you my number and you can call me when you are ready."

Smooth, Ken. Give her an out, the no-pressure sales pitch. She jotted down his number and they were both on their way. He heading into work on a Friday night, and she home to relax after a long work week.

His head was spinning as he drove into the depot. The scattered thoughts were not remnants from the ice chunk to the head, not directly anyway. What are the odds of all this being a coincidence? He hadn't seen Jane Warner since graduation. She pops up in great detail during a trip back in time, and upon his return she walks into his world. What forces are at work? It was time for Ken's first call into *Across the Globe*. David Sphere would surely be interested in talking about this experience.

HELLO DAVID SPHERE

"Good to see you back, Ken. You look good."

"Try as you might, Bill, you couldn't kill me. My head is too hard!"

They laughed at each other. Ken liked to make people laugh, often at his own expense. They had met in Bill's small office. This night Ken did something he never did. He shut the door of his boss's office. He had to get something off his chest.

"Holy crap, Ken, here it comes! You're shutting the door. You're really gonna let me have it. I thought we agreed it was an accident." Powers was being sarcastic, but he was actually surprised, not sure what Ken had in mind.

"Bill, I think you did me a favor."

"I did? How is that?"

"Without getting into a long play-by-play, I'll tell you what happened. Very odd stuff, really surreal." Ken had no desire to start a drawn-out diatribe about time travel. The Cliffs Notes version would be sufficient for his buddy Bill.

"I will keep this short. We have work to do tonight. Bill, sit back and take this in. After I got knocked out in the lot, I found myself in my old neighborhood, back in high school. Like a dream, but with so much detail. The people, places, cars, music, all of it. I was there, Bill, right there. I don't have dreams like that and haven't since that night. This dream just kept going, getting more detailed from one day to the next."

"That is odd. I never had a dream that went on for more than a day. Usually it is just a moment, a small event. So you think the coma brought this on?"

"My neurologist says the brain shouldn't work that way; your thoughts just shut down. But he did say that some patients woke up and said things similar to what I did. Anyway, to get to the important part, I saw a lot of people from my past: grandparents, parents, teachers, coaches. I also saw this girl I didn't really know in school, other than her name. She was smart, very studious. Always polite. Struck me as a real decent person. But back then that wasn't what we were looking for."

"Sure, you're skirt chasing back then."

"And flying blind, clueless. In this dream I chat her up, put some light moves on her. Nothing creepy, mind you. This isn't a teenage lust dream."

"I hope not, Ken. I wouldn't want the details if it was!" Powers was laughing again.

"No, nothing like that. I just took the opportunity to approach someone I should have back in the day. Bill, it was so damn real, the conversation, the way she looked, everything. I had never talked to this girl in the real world."

No need to ramble on with the nitty gritty about his trip to the 1980s. Ken moved on.

"One of the things I took away from the time I was out, dreaming, was you should take a chance when something feels right. Get after it. So this is the odd part. I am on my way to work tonight, stopped at the mini-mart, and..."

"And there she was."

"You got it. I guess with the lead-up I was giving away the ending of the story."

"Right, kid, and it looks like someone is trying to tell you something. What did you do when you saw her?"

"I asked her out on a date."

"That's it! That's my boy! What did she say?"

"I gave her my phone number and told her to call me to confirm. I didn't want to be too pushy and lean on her for her number. It would have looked like kid stuff."

"Smooth move, Ken, classy. She'll call, if she's single. Even if she isn't, a dinner date is not a big deal, unless she shows up with her boyfriend or husband! If that is the case, make him pick up half of the bill. It is only fair!" Now they were both laughing.

"She wasn't wearing any rings and didn't say anything about a boyfriend or husband, but who knows, I may never hear back."

"She'll call. Trust me."

"What makes you so sure?"

"You're a good-looking guy, a nice fella. Like I said, I would let my daughter date you. If I had one."

"So, Bill, looks like you knocked some sense into me. But you almost killed me to get your point across. How about going a little easier with your advice!"

"Hey, it worked, didn't it?" Bill was smiling ear to ear.

"We will see. We can talk more later. Work calls, my friend."

"Shouldn't I be the one telling you that?" The sign-off was Bill's often repeated line.

***

Getting back into the swing of things wasn't difficult. It's not as if they were trekking to Mars. The work routine, but necessary. As the late hours rolled in, things often slowed. Ken sat in the cab of his truck, knowing what he wanted to do. It was time for his first call-in to *Across the Globe*. Ken's little adventure should be worth David Sphere's time. It was Open-Line Friday – whatever the callers wanted to talk about, within bounds. This wasn't relationship-fixing or car talk time. The topic should be along the paranormal or conspiracy lines. For David Sphere and his listeners, Ken's adventure would be right up their alley.

Ken didn't want to give too much information. The calls were on a first-name only basis. He simply had to say what coast he was calling from. He'd be "Ken from the East Coast." No need for more than that. Nobody knew he was a listener, especially at the depot. His co-workers were not into the show, not their speed. He would spend his lunch break with David Sphere.

Ken got through right away. He realized the show wasn't wildly popular, but he didn't think he would be on the air so quickly. He calmly told the call screener it was his first time calling in and he wanted to talk about dream interpretation. The screener liked the idea and pushed Ken up to the front of the line. Ken was a bit nervous, having never called into any radio show.

"Hello, Ken from the East Coast, you are on Open-Line Friday. What would you like to talk about?"

"Wow, I got on quick, David! First-time caller, not just to you, but to anyone."

"Great! We must be doing something right!"

"You are, David, and I want to say right away, thank you. For those of us who work overnights, you are good company. No one is screaming at anyone on this program. It is respectful."

"Ken, that is exactly what we aim for. Dialogue, no yelling."

"To be completely upfront, I am not, at least I wasn't before, a paranormal type or a conspiracy fan. I am a cut-and-dry sort, boring really."

"And have we changed that, Ken? Maybe opened up your mind a bit?"

"Yes and no. I am still boring, but there is one particular topic that caught my attention, something you don't cover as much."

"And what is that, Ken?"

"Time travel. I think some of the theories are interesting. With what I've heard discussed, it moves the topic out of the science fiction scenario and into the world of real science. I still don't think it can be done with our current capabilities, but it got me thinking."

"Yes, Ken, I would say 'theoretically possible,' but it ain't happening. At least not yet."

"Not literally, David, no, but…"

"You have something to share, Ken?"

Ken was hesitant. He didn't want to get into personal circumstances. He also didn't want any of the other listeners to recognize him, but he felt that would be unlikely. Who the heck does he know that would listen to this show?

"I will be quick, David, give you the abbreviated version of what happened to me."

"Please do. We would love to hear it."

"I was involved in a workplace accident, got knocked unconscious and ended up in the ICU."

"Sorry to hear that, Ken. I hope you're OK now."

"Yeah, back up and running, all good, but something happened when I was out. I had a vivid dream. Not several, but one long, involved, detailed dream."

"Really, and you remember it all, you know what happened?"

"Play by play. That is very odd, not typical for me. It was like I was there, back in time, the sights, sounds, people, smells, colors."

"We have heard that from people who have been out for a while, unconscious. Lucid dreams is a phrase that is used to describe the event."

"I can say this, David, if it wasn't time travel, it was the next best thing. I'm telling you I was there, maybe only in my mind, but I was there."

"The mind is amazing, isn't it?"

"Yes, and that is why I called in. I wanted to say that regardless of how real or not real the experience was, it can be used to help people. Your brain is trying to tell you something. Something may be right in front of you, and you don't see. But your inner brain does. It is trying to help you, and as long as it isn't telling you to mount a tower with a rifle, you may want to listen."

"Hah, yes, right you are, Ken! As long as you are getting good advice, take it!"

"Exactly. I may have a date coming up thanks to that dream, or time travel, or whatever it was."

"Isn't that something. I'm not going to dig into that, Ken, sounds personal, but it looks like it worked out for you."

"Yeah, bad accident leads to quasi-real event and maybe something positive comes out of it all. Mysterious stuff for sure. My grandmother used to say the Lord acts in mysterious ways. Who knows what will happen."

"Ken, I would say the best we can do is to do the things right now that we would have done if we had the chance to go back. Does that make sense?"

Ken was already doing that. "David, it makes perfect sense."

"We're are coming up on a hard break. Thank you for the call, Ken."

"Thank you, David. You make the midnight shift more interesting."

"Good night, Ken. Don't be afraid to call back and let us know how the date goes."

Sphere was joking. He was far from a love-line talk show host. No way was Ken calling back and discussing a date over the phone, putting more of his private life out to the public. He went beyond what he had wanted to say. He'd intended to keep quiet about the date, but it slipped out. His nerves got the better of him. But it had all been harmless enough. Back to work now. There were trailers to move around the yard.

* * *

Ken made it through his first night back with ease. Overall, a good night's work, and he managed to get in a call to David Sphere. Skipper greeted him at the door, waiting on his morning walk. The dog got spoiled when Ken was at home recovering, enjoying multiple long walks each day. Now with his master back on the clock, their walks would become less frequent. Such is a dog's life.

After the morning stroll, Ken hit the sack and was out in no time, sleeping like a baby. He awoke to the sound of his phone a little after noon. He didn't recognize the number on caller ID, which would usually be a cue to not pick up, a telemarketer likely on the other end. But there was another possibility. He had to answer the call.

"Hello." Ken's voice was groggy.

"Hi Ken, did I wake you?" It was Jane.

"No big deal. I worked last night, midnight shift. I get up around now anyway. You did me a favor."

"When I started at the lab, we had a full overnight shift. I was assigned to it. It killed me, such a long night. I have been on days for years. Now they have a skeleton crew on nights. Some people like it. The quiet I guess."

"Yeah, I am planning on moving to days. I have done nights for long enough. I am becoming nocturnal."

There was a moment of silence before Jane spoke again. Ken was still getting his bearings after his slumber. Skipper had heard talking on the phone and came in to investigate.

"If you still want to go out for dinner or lunch, I am up for it."

"Great, Jane, absolutely. You know, lunch sounds like a nice idea. Less hassle, smaller crowd, I am a big lunch guy."

"When were you thinking about going?"

"Jane, we could go today, catch a late lunch, if you aren't doing anything."

Ken was hungry, and why not move while he had her on the line. No time better than now.

"Ok, sure, I don't have anything going on. You still into the Olive Garden?" She didn't sound particularly enthused about the menu at the Italian chain restaurant.

"I was kidding, Jane, a little nervous banter. I tend to do that when lurking outside the window of a woman's car parked in a mini-mart parking lot."

"Ha, ha, I figured that."

"You pick the place and I'll be there."

"How about the Villa, downtown. It shouldn't be too crowded. The food is great. It was my grandparents' favorite spot. They took me there all the time."

"Jane, you can't go wrong with a grandparents' pick. I am familiar with the place, never ate there though. What time is good?"

"You just got up, so…"

"Give me an hour and a half. I can shower quick and meet you there."

"Sounds like a plan. Ken, I do have a question for you."

Oh, here it comes. What did she find out about Ken Heet? Hopefully nothing too awkward.

"Sure. What's up?"

"Were you on the radio last night?"

Holy crap! What are the chances? You have to be kidding me. Come clean Ken. She caught you.

"Well, yeah, yes, and I can't believe anyone other than midnight dwellers listens to that! You seem too normal."

"Ha, ha, I told you I worked the midnight shift. That is the only thing I found remotely interesting on those long overnight shifts. I would get done with my work halfway through the night. I had to do something."

"Wow, and you still listen?"

"Not often. I was up late last night, couldn't sleep. I put on David Sphere to knock me out."

"And you heard Ken from the East Coast calling in."

"Yep, and if I hadn't met you at the store, I would have never known who it was."

"True story, Jane. I got clobbered at work, went into a deep sleep, had a long, vivid dream, and got some good advice from my grandparents. That's the long and short of it."

That was enough for now. Ken could tell her more if things went well. No way was he going to say, 'I met you in my dreams.' That would be too much too soon. It could spook her.

"Well, grandparents can offer some great advice, no doubt about it."

"Sure enough. So, see you at two o'clock."

"Absolutely. Don't rush, Ken. I will wait in the lounge for you."

"Great. See you soon."

Ken hung up with a smile. Things just keep getting more surreal.

"Skipper, let's take a walk. Your boy has a date."

Out they went for an abbreviated walk. Ken had places to be, and a special someone to see. Who knows what would become of this, but the coincidences were piling up. What a strange, strange world it is. He and Skipper trotted down the street, one as happy as the other. Who knew what awaited, perhaps things were finally coming together.

* * *

One of the most important questions that can be asked is: How much time do we have? Most often there is no definitive answer. The best a person can do is put what time is in front of them to good use. To constantly rehash what has come to pass is to waste the time still available.

Most of Jane Warner's goals had been crossed off. Now she sat in a laboratory wondering what was next. She could come and go and was well compensated, but the antiseptic environment of the lab had become a prison of sorts. Was this quality time? She thought not.

Ken Heet's lab was the cab of a tractor-trailer. The closest Ken came to scientific study was *Across the Globe* – questionable research for sure. But the former high school classmates found themselves in very similar situations. They were both alone, looking for more out of life. The two shared noble characteristics, both being dedicated, honest, and reliable. Such traits are to be admired and the foundation of any relationship. Two people who appeared dissimilar, were actually two peas in a pod.

Ken and Jane couldn't reclaim past time. There are no trips back in time, despite what the experts on David Sphere's program might say. The two former classmates now had a chance for a future together in an uncertain world. Better late than never. They now had a chance to share the most precious commodity. Their time was now.

Acknowledgments

Thanks to those who helped make this book possible

Julia H. Casey for adding shine to the finished product.

Danny and Finn Casey for providing a ringside seat
to the world of scholastic sports programs.

Robert Brill for a thorough edit and great conversation.

Jill Giulietti, a great Texan who provided
eye catching graphic art work.

A special thanks to Patricia Hommel who takes the time
to read everything I write. An arduous task for sure!